Perpetrator
Transformed from Selfish to Selfless to Servant

Vernel Edwards

Entegrity Choice Publishing
PO Box 453
Powder Springs, GA 30127
info@entegritypublishing.com

Book Cover Designed by:
Jodilyn Solace
www.highrealmgraphics.com

ISBN: 978-0-9909397-7-1
ISBN: 978-0-9909397-6-4 (eBook)

Library of Congress Control Number: 2015950744

Printed in the United States of America

To my beloved mother,
thanks for your encouraging last words to me.
I will never forget them. Love always!

Acknowledgments

To my beloved father, mother, and brothers, who will always be remembered. Mr. Vernel Edwards, Mrs. Lossie Pompey, Andrew, and Areatess, I miss you. To my siblings left to keep the family strong—Caroline, William, Calvin, Brenda, Linda, Johnny, and Jackie—thanks for everything.

Special thanks to:
- My Christian sisters Adriene Thorpe, Carol Lyles, Crystal Evans, and Sarah Middleton, for helping me stay focused and encouraged.
- Ministers Yvonne Fredericks, Sara Smith, and Sandra Walker, for being the first ones to read *Perpetrator*. I will never forget your kindness and how you confirmed what God was doing through me.
- Reverends Richard and Maxine Johnson, my spiritual parents, who continuously pray for my spiritual growth.
- Reverend Dr. Charles Jackson, Sr. for preaching and teaching God's word.
- Reverend Dr. Hazel Wilson, Reverend Alison Baker, and Tyrone Brown, your thoughtfulness will always be remembered.

Thanks to my daughter Shantel, my son-in law Kamau, and my grandsons Khalil and Kaymen for always believing in me.

Foreword

I have been inspired to write many Christian songs, including "You Say". I knew instantly this song was different from all the songs I had been blessed to write thus far.

The words of this song inspired me to think of a movie. Within two weeks, the outline of the movie was written. When I prayed about the title, I was inspired to entitle it *Perpetrator*. As I finished the movie, my dear sister in Christ, Carol Lyles said, I should write the book first. So I began the journey of writing this book and found myself excited. All along the way, I felt God's love, peace, and confirmation that I was on his path.

When I started to seek the most appropriate way to explain the title (*Perpetrator*), God blessed me to have a conversation with a matriarch in my life, Ms. Glenice Pearson. She shared with me her view of what it means to have a relationship with God. I totally agreed with what she said, and it sums up what I feel is appropriate to lead me into an explanation of *Perpetrator*.

"When you consider yourself as having a relationship with God," she said, "a few thoughts should come to mind:

- "It's personal; there is no formula. All come to love him through some life experience.
- "It's forever developing.
- "It depends on your faith, your trust in him, and your desire for him.
- "It's shaped by individual experiences.
- "It's an understanding that you made the personal choice to have a relationship with him because he pursued you.
- "It's good.
- "It's worth it! All who have nurtured a serious relationship with God will emphatically agree; it's worth it!

- "And there will be some sign in a person's life that he or she has entered into a true relationship with God."

Perpetrator, as it relates to this book, is the exact opposite of Glenice's espousal on having a true relationship with God. It is an outward form of a relationship with God, intermingled with self-centered desires that reek of the attitude that "I will serve God on my terms."

Why is this a problem? Most notable is the false balance this perpetrator represents. And a false balance is an abomination before God, who knows what's in a man's heart. To have an outward form of a relationship with God, intermingled with self-centered desires, serves no purpose but to set in motion the preparation for you to reap what you have sown.

Still, God stands at the door of your heart and knocks so that he can bring you to his expected end. Take the *Perpetrator* journey. Make sure you look within for self-centeredness. Don't deny it, if it's in you, but rather, choose God's path of selflessness to become a servant. And allow him to lead you on your journey to enlightenment, encouragement, and an awesome relationship with him.

Contents

Author's Note

Perpetrator has three main characters whose stories are told in the following order: Constance Wilts, Baryy Greene, and Vonder Staten. Each character's story is written independent of the stories of the others, and based in the 1980s and 1990s. The last chapter, entitled "Religiosity Revealed," allows the reader to experience more of each character's brokenness and takes the reader on a journey to discover how all three of them experience a way to escape.

Chapter 1
What a Mother

In a rural and swampy area of Suffolk, Virginia, stands a small wooden building that is centered on two acres of land. It is 10:30 AM on a Sunday morning, and inside this building, a church service is drawing to an end. The preached word has almost the entire congregation on their feet—some are clapping; some are shouting; others are smiling and even crying.

The one thing they all have in common is the fanning. All styles and types of fans are waving in the air, because this building has no air conditioning, and the eighty-eight degree air inside feels like one hundred degrees.

June Duval, a beautiful young woman is sitting quietly amidst the excitement in the front pew, directly in front of the pulpit, with her seven-year-old daughter, Constance Wilts.

Marvin Anderson Sr. is fervently preaching, as sweat drips from his brow. He completes his sermon, raises his hands, and blesses the congregation. He closes with the doxology, stares at the young woman, scans the congregation one last time, and then says, "Be blessed; I'll see y'all back here next Sunday."

Before exiting through a side door, he stares at the young woman one last time.

The young woman hurriedly picks up her purse and says to her daughter, "Stay here. I'll be back."

She walks to the side door through which the preacher exited, looks back at her daughter, and brings her finger to her mouth. Then she stretches out her hand, signifying to the child that she should be quiet and not move. As soon as the mother opens the side door, the child stands up and follows her. She watches as her mom enters the room in the back of the church. She sits on the floor with her back to the wall, right across from the door. She wraps her arms around her legs, puts her chin on her knees, and waits. After a long while, her mother exits the room.

She opens the door, while looking back, and saying, "I'll call you later honey", as she places a rolled up amount of cash in her purse. After closing the door, she looks down and sees her daughter. She says, "I told you to stay where you were. Why did you move?"

The daughter replies, "I wanted to come with you."

Her mother stares at her for a minute, thinking about what she said. She leans down, grabs her daughter's hand, pulls her up, and then they walk away.

*　*　*

"Please, Mama, don't make me go," twelve-year-old Constance begs, as she stands in front of the bathroom mirror with her mother, June.

June quickly finishes curling Constance's hair, and then she straightens the straps on Constance's low-cut, black, fitted dress, to make sure she meets her approval.

"It's survival of the fittest, honey," June replies, as she squeezes the pump on a bottle of perfume, allowing its mist to shower Constance's neck and chest.

"I know, but I don't wanna go," Constance continues pleading.

"Want to go" June corrects her. "Remember, you need to talk proper."

"We've talked about this," June responds with a sharp voice, and then she says, "Turn around." Constance looks up at her mom with tears in her eyes and then turns her back. "Constance! No," June says, while misting her back with the perfume. "I know how you feel; I used to feel the same way, but its okay. You'll be okay."

June gently turns Constance around and wipes her tears. They walk out the front door of their old, run-down trailer and get into their Volkswagen. Night has fallen as they drive to the back of a building and park directly in front of the door.

"Mama, please?" Constance says as she leans toward her mother and looks at her.

June replies, "Constance, open the door and get out now. You can't be late; this costs us money that we need."

Constance opens the door and steps out of the car. June is already standing at the front of the car, reaching for her hand. She pulls Constance along beside her as she walks up to the back door and rings the bell. A tall man with a bald head opens the door. Blues music blasts in the background as he says in a deep voice, "Y'all almost late."

"Almost, but not quite," June replies as she pushes Constance in the door, next to the tall man, and says, "I'll be back in two hours."

She turns and walks to her car, gets in, and sits for a moment, looking at her watch. The time is eight o'clock. She looks at the back door, which the man has now closed, starts her car, and drives away.

* * *

Ten years later, Constance is now a young woman, twenty-two years old. She is five feet, one inch tall, 105 pounds, with a petite, curvaceous body; her light brown eyes compliment her golden brown skin. She now has a ten-year-old brother, Jim Duval. She and Jim have been summoned to the living room by their mother.

Constance sits on a worn, blue velvet chair. One of the arms has been wrapped with tape to keep it from falling off. She stares at her mother (an older version of herself, with thirty extra pounds and light green eyes), with her lips pouted and a frown on her face. June is sitting on a three-cushion sofa with big blue and orange flowers that have faded over time. Jim (a scrawny kid with eyes like his mother) sits directly in front of his mother on a black footstool that has rips and white cushion exposed.

The room is silent, and nobody seems to want to be there. Jim fumbles with the cup in his hand as he looks down at the floor, refusing to look at his mother. June holds her forehead, looks back and forth at each child, but remains silent. Constance is antsy; her chair squeaks as she leans from side to side, waiting to hear what her mother has to say, although she's sure she already knows what's coming.

Still looking back and forth at each child, June finally says, "Now listen. I need you, and you may not think so, but you need me too." Shaking her head, June continues, "A real family stay togetha. We gonna make it. I know it. Let's put our head togetha and see what we need to do to get over this hump."

June looks at Jim and asks, "You got yards to cut this week, right? I'm gonna need money from you for food." Then she turns her face toward Constance and says, "I need you to take care of rent."

Constance sighs and turns her face away from her mother for a moment. Then she looks at her again in disgust and says, "I can't take this no mo. Ma, you lost your job again? How?"

Jim mumbles. Constance looks at him as he drops his head and says, "I need my money." He stands up and throws his cup against the wall. Both Constance and June look at him in shock as he walks out of the room. Constance quickly looks again at her mother and says, "I'm sick of being somebody's fantasy toy in the back room of strip clubs all over town because you can't keep a real job."

June does not answer Constance. She continues looking in the direction of the door where Jim left the room and shouts, "Boy, you lost your mind? Get back here!"

Constance stares at the door until Jim reappears. When her eyes catch his, she smiles at him and shakes her head from side to side as if to say, "Don't say anything. Stay calm." For a moment she continues to smile at Jim, until she hears June say, "I tell you … all I done for y'all since you were born, and this is the thanks I get. Constance! Constance!"

After hearing her name shouted twice, Constance finally looks at her mother.

"How I lost my job is not the issue; how we keep a roof over our heads is. Now do what I taught you, and get what we need. Understand?" June says.

Constance knows her mother wants her to blossom into a seductive night prowler, find some man, and sweep him off his feet by servicing him. Her mother says it's all about the survival of the fittest.

Constance lowers her voice and says, "Ma, it's over. I'm leavin' for good, I swear. I'm not gonna let you use me like this." Then she stares at June and cocks her head to the side.

"Use you?" June says. "I don't believe what I'm hearing. Plenty children go out they way to help they ma in time of need, and I end up with two of the most ungrateful people in the world. Use you?"

June continues to speak but Constance stands up and walks past Jim, who is still standing in the doorway. She hears June dismiss Jim by yelling, "Get outta my sight!"

Constance makes her way to her bedroom and closes the door. She walks over to her closet, takes out her large luggage bag, and throws it on her bed. She opens the bag, then goes over to her four drawer dresser. She starts pulling clothes out of her dresser. Without looking, she throws the clothes in the direction of her bag on the bed. She empties all her drawers and then walks over to her closet. She pulls her clothes off their hangers and throws them in the direction of her bag too. Her bed and bag are now loaded with clothing. She walks over to her bed, pulls her hair back out of her face, sorts through her clothes, lays an outfit to the side, and then begins stuffing all the clothing into the bag before zipping it closed.

Straining, she pulls the bag to the floor and stands it upright on its two wheels. She makes her way to the bathroom and takes a shower.

June is still sitting in the living room. She pops the cap off a twenty-ounce beer and gulps it down. Jim is in his room, sitting on the bed, slowly bouncing his basketball between his legs. June quickly finishes her beer and is about to open a second can when she hears the doorbell.

She walks to the door and opens it. Instantly, she smiles and gives a tall, slim man a big hug.

"Hey honey, I didn't expect to see you today," she says. The man is her new lover, Paul.

He smiles as he hugs her and says, "Come on, take a ride with me."

June and Paul walk down the front steps to his car. Constance has just made it back into her room. She looks out the window and watches her mother and Paul drive away. Constance quickly dresses and walks to her mother's room. She enters the room, walks over to the dresser, and opens the top drawer. She lifts up the clothing and picks up a little black address book. Then she sits on the bed with the book in her hand. She sits and flips through the pages, looking at all the names in the address book.

She thinks back to when she was twelve years old and she saw her mother holding the little black book open, staring at one of the pages. She had asked her mother what was in the book.

"Nothin' you need to know," her mother said, and she placed the book back in her dresser drawer.

Constance looked at the book and thought to herself, *What's the big deal? It's just an address book.*

When she returns from her deep thoughts, she says to the address book, "You my ticket to freedom. I'm no longa a slave."

She gets up from the bed and walks back to her room. She kneels down and pulls a glass jar from under her bed. She opens it and pulls out a wad of cash wrapped in a rubber band. She looks at it and says, "Survival of the fittest," as she picks up her purse, drops the wad of cash inside, and closes it. She leaves her room, pulling the bag down the hall toward the front door. As she walks past Jim's room, she sees him sitting on his bed and stops in the doorway. She stands the bag up, sets her purse and the address book on top of it, and walks into Jim's room. He doesn't look at her. She sits next to him on his bed and watches him bounce his basketball between his legs.

"Jim, I—"

Jim cuts her off and says, "You ain't comin' back." He still does not look at her.

She grabs his ball, holds it, and tells him, "I swear, I am." She attempts to turn his face toward her, but he pulls away. "I love you," she says. "I'll neva forget about you. I swear." She places his basketball back in his lap and walks to the door. When she looks back, she notices that Jim is still not looking at her.

She picks up the address book and places it in her purse. Then she hangs her purse on her shoulder, rolls the luggage bag to the front door, and walks outside and down the porch, rolling her bag slowly off each step.

The sun is slowly going down as Constance rolls her bag down the country road. She struggles with pulling the bag and holding her purse. She moves the purse from one shoulder to the other as she continues walking the five miles into town.

Day turns to evening, and she nears the dreary swamp area with its earthy smell; the road is especially dark and quiet. She is nervous, but she never stops walking and pulling the luggage bag along beside her. She tries to hold her breath as she walks, but she realizes that that makes her even more tired and anxious. She looks from side to side and then in front and back of her as she walks as fast as she can, struggling with the bag. The bag wheels make loud noises as she pulls it along, but she can hear all of the strange night sounds in spite of the wheels.

As she walks, most of the night sounds make her jump. She knows this is a desperate move, because no one she has ever known has walked the long, swampy road at night, not even guys. But she is determined to leave her mother's controlling ways behind her; she sucks up her fears and fatigue and keeps walking. "Thank you, God," she says as she walks along. When she gets to the end of the swampy area, she gets a little pep in her step and smiles as she makes her way into town.

Finally she reaches the bus station. Exhausted, she opens the station door and looks around. The place is small and filled to capacity. People are standing on the walls because there are no chairs. The place is full of chatter from all the conversations. The door closes behind her as she inhales deeply, then exhales slowly. Her eyes scan the room, looking for a vacant seat. She notices people staring at her but pays them no attention. An old lady sitting in the corner motions to her to come over. She has no idea what this lady wants but starts walking toward her, pulling her bag very carefully, making sure not to bump anyone's legs.

When Constance gets to the old lady, she says, "You can have my seat, honey." She stands up, puts her purse on her shoulder, and walks away. Constance looks around the room at the people standing on the wall and wonders why the lady called her over. She hears someone say, "I've been standing for thirty minutes." She pouts her lips at them and sits down, making sure to pull her bag close to her. Her feet are hurting and she does not care how long they have been standing.

She takes her purse off her shoulder, pulls out the address book, and flips the pages one by one, looking at all the names. After flipping five pages, she notices the name Mae at the top of the page. The name and information catch her eyes. She cocks her head to the side, thinking about her second cousin Mae, and decides that's who she is going to call. She stands her bag directly in front of the chair and then makes her way to the counter to ask the attendant if she can use the phone. He looks her up and down, and then he hands it to her, while pointing at the sign on the wall that reads, "Local Calls Only."

She smiles at him. When he turns to assist another customer, she dials the long distance number. Mae answers with a friendly voice. When Constance hears Mae's voice, she swallows and the knot in her throat releases; she says, "Cousin Mae, its Constance."

She waits for a response. Mae says with enthusiasm, "Oh my God, Constance? How are you?"

Constance replies, "Fine," as she holds the phone, smiling, and looks upward, mouthing a silent "Thank you, God." Constance continues, "I'd like to come for a visit."

Mae answers, "Please do. When can you come?"

Constance says, "I can leave out today, if that's okay?"

Mae says, Of course it is."

Constance tells Mae she will be arriving on the bus and will call her when she gets in town.

She hands the man the phone, thanks him, and says, "I need a ticket to New Orleans please; when is the next bus leavin'?"

"That will be one hundred seventy-five dollars one way, three hundred dollars round trip," the attendant says. "Next bus leaves at six tomorrow morning."

Constance hands the attendant cash and looks up at the clock on the wall. It is eight o'clock. The attendant hands her a ticket, and she thanks him and walks back to her seat.

Constance looks up toward heaven again and closes her eyes for a moment, thanking God for the little black book and the bus ticket. She sits down and looks around the station. As each hour passes, she watches people leave the room. By eleven o'clock, the station is empty, except for her and the attendant on duty. She sits quietly. As she feels herself falling asleep, she places her purse behind her back. The attendant notices she's asleep but doesn't bother her.

By early morning, she's awakened by a baby crying. She looks around the room and notices that a woman is sitting two rows to the left of her with a newborn baby. She sees an older man standing at the counter, talking with another attendant. She grabs her purse from behind her back, opens it quickly, and counts her cash. She closes it and lifts it up to her chest, and then she looks at the clock on the wall; it's five o'clock. She realizes she's been asleep for several hours. She looks again at the attendant standing at the counter and realizes she slept through a shift change. She makes her way to the ladies room and freshens up, and then she goes back to her seat. At six o'clock, she gets in line with several others, waiting to take their seats on the bus to New Orleans.

As she steps onto the bus, she smiles at the driver. He's an older man with a large round stomach. He's balding in the top of his head with hair around the sides. He looks her up and down while smiling back at her. She thinks to herself, Excuse you, huh, and walks to the back of the bus. "Perfect," she says in a soft voice as she sits down and slides over to the window. After the last person takes their seat, the driver stands up and starts speaking. She pays him no attention and looks out her window. Her thoughts go to the family reunion she and her mother had attended when she was six years old. At the reunion, Mae expressed an interest in her coming for a visit or even for the entire summer, but June would not agree to any length of time.

"Enjoy the ride," the driver says as he takes his seat and starts the engine. Constance continues thinking about Mae. In her mind, Mae is the family member she needs at this time in her life.

She thinks about what her first words will be when she sees Mae. She is confident that whatever she says, if she says it in the right way, it will be good enough to get the results she wants. Since she has been old enough to talk, her mother has coached her in how to manipulate people, and Constance knows she has perfected it.

Constance realizes she doesn't know her family. She wonders if anyone knows what she has been exposed to by her mother. The bus travels pass several cars on the road and quickly shifts lanes, causing everyone to lean in their seats.

Constance rolls her eyes at the back of the driver's head and says in a low voice, "I hope this idiot don't get us killed." She returns to her thoughts and shakes her head, thinking, *All my life I've watched Ma use her friends and so many men. I'm tired of moving from one run-down place to another.* Constance knows Mae prays for June to change. She has heard June tell her friends, "I don't go to church often but my cousin Mae always prays for me, want me to change, but I'm not."

The sign on the road changes from Highway 95 to Route 20 west. Constance falls asleep. She wakes up when the bus stops. The driver says, "This stop is Alabama. Refresh yourself and we'll pull out in fifteen minutes."

Constance exits the bus along with everyone else and makes her way to the restroom. After washing up, she gets back on board, and the bus starts up again. Day turns to evening as the bus travels on. Constance is anxious to get to Mae's home; she hopes Mae invites her to move in with her. She knows the call she made to Mae at the bus station was only to ask if she could come for a visit, but she wants her visit to last beyond a few days or weeks. She hates the thought of leaving Jim behind to deal with their mother's lifestyle alone, but she feels she will go insane if she stays another day.

Her real desire is to be a career woman and live the life of a respectable young lady. Although she graduated from high school, she has many problems. She has limited job skills, no money, and only her mother's way of life as her source of income. All she knows is what her mother has taught her since she was a child: how to manipulate everyone, especially men, to get what she wants.

June perfected the art of using people. From the time Constance was a little girl, her mother has used people; there were many men in and out of their home. Paul, June's new lover, is another preacher—much younger than the one she dated when Constance was seven years old—and he really cares for her. June has been successful in fooling him by pretending to be in love with Jesus. And although Constance does not like her mother's ways, like an old pro, she has perfected the image of being in love with Jesus.

Chapter 2
Away from It All or Not?

Constance arrives in New Orleans at the bus station. She hails a taxi. While the taxi driver is loading her bag in the trunk, she opens the right side, back passenger door and gets in. The driver gets in and ask "Where to?" She calls out Mae's address, from the address book. The driver wisp away, taking her to Mae's home. She looks out the back of the taxi at the people and the townhouses along the way. When the driver pulls on to Mae's street, she notices that it is a middle class neighborhood where all the homes look the same. He stops in front of Mae's home. Constance steps out of the car and waits for the driver to get her luggage bag out of the trunk.

After she pays him, she turns around and sees a beautiful woman standing on the porch, smiling at her. She smiles back and says, "Hello, Cousin Mae."

Mae says, "Oh my God, Constance, I am so glad to see you." Mae stretches out her arms to hug Constance as she walks up onto the porch. They embrace for a moment and then Mae says, "Come on in."

Constance follows Mae into the kitchen and sits at the table. The kitchen is very spacious and well decorated with pictures of fruit on the walls and utensils hanging from the ceiling around a center island range. The small table Constance sits at is right next to a beautiful bay window with a view of Mae's rose garden.

Mae, a retired teacher, stands at the range, turning it on to boil water for tea. She is in her late sixties, tall and slim with long hair; she is very soft-spoken.

Constance looks out the window at the beautiful garden. The sun reflects off Constance's face, giving her a glow and highlighting her facial expressions. Constance has strategically positioned herself at the table so Mae sees her sitting with her elbows on the table, fingers intertwined, and looking out the window with a blank stare.

She looks in Mae's direction and says, "Thanks for letting me come."

"Honey, you're always welcome in my home," Mae says. "I am so glad you're finally here. Now tell me, how are you doing?"

"I've been going to church and learning so much about God. I'm sold out for Jesus. I love him with all my heart. God said, 'Seek ye first the kingdom of God, and his righteousness; and all these things shall be added unto you,' and that's how I feel. I don't want anything but to know God for myself and serve him."

With a big smile on her face, Mae places two teacups on the counter, and then she turns toward Constance and says, "I would have to say my prayers have been getting through. I am so glad to hear you talk like this. You have no idea how I pray for you and your family. How are your mother and brother?"

Constance drops her head as though ashamed.

"Fine, just fine," she says. She waits for a moment and then says, "Well, I'm tryin' to have my own life. I'm sicka her."

Mae looks as though she is in shock.

"What is the problem?"

The sun illuminates the one tear rolling down Constance's cheek as she says in a soft voice, "Ma. She can't keep a job. Every time she gets one, she loses it, and ..." Constance sighs and then says, "I can't do nothing for myself. I wanna save some money so I can move out, but I have to support her. Every time I mention leavin', she starts with her sob story 'bout how she needs me, and I need her. I can't take it." Constance wipes her cheek and returns to staring blankly out the window. After a period of silence, she speaks again while still looking out the window. "God is callin' me to a higher place, and I wanna know him for myself." She looks at Mae again. "I'm steppin' out on faith and trustin' God that I can make it on my own." Constance looks sad, drops her head, and continues, "I don't know how. But I know I can."

Mae is completely taken in by Constance's actions. She walks over to Constance and places her hand on Constance's shoulder. "You are no longer a kid," she says. "You need to move out."

Constance now has tears running down both cheeks.

Mae takes a seat next to Constance and says, "Oh honey, you will make it if you want. You are welcome to stay here with me. Don't worry about a thing; God always provides for those who are his." Smiling, Mae says, "I'm proud of you." Mae's facial expression turns serious as she continues, "Your mother needs prayer more than she needs you."

Constance smiles and extends her arms to hug Mae.

"Thanks, Cousin Mae," she says.

The tea kettle whistles as she and Mae hug. Mae stands up, walks over to the range, picks up the kettle, and then looks back at Constance and says, "Let's have our tea."

Constance's first three weeks with Mae went by fast. Each week they went to Sunday morning service, Wednesday Bible study, and Thursday prayer service. In between their church attendance, they spent time talking and drinking tea. Mae told Constance how the family hated the fact that June moved away from everyone and never came back to visit, not even her own siblings and parents. Mae showed Constance pictures of the family in her photo albums. Some of them Constance could remember from her two or three childhood visits to family reunions. Constance told Mae about her mother's lifestyle and how they had to move often. Mae already knew some of what Constance shared, but she was appalled at what Constance had been through.

After a month with Mae, Constance had grown tired of their routine. One Sunday after service, Constance asked one of the church members if they knew where she could get a job. The young lady told her the convenience store near Mae's home was hiring. On the drive home, Constance says to Mae, "I heard the convenience store down the street is hiring. I'll go down tomorrow and apply."

Mae says, "Honey, I don't think that's a good idea." She looks at Constance and then says, "I understand you need a job, but that's just such a dangerous place to work."

Constance says, "I've been through worse." Constance applied the next day and started work on Tuesday. Her schedule did not allow her to attend Wednesday Bible study or Thursday prayer service. She was okay with that, although she told Mae she felt terrible about it. By her third month with Mae, her work schedule prevented her from attending church all together. She mainly worked nights and weekends and had weekdays off.

One day, Mae shares with Constance that she thought of her as the daughter she never had. Mae tells her she misses them attending church together, adding that she would help her find a new job so they could get back to their routine.

Constance agrees, knowing that's what Mae wants to hear, but she has no intention of attending church again. Constance was tired and ready to leave Mae's house. She makes plans for her departure. She knows she needs money to move on. When Mae leaves home one day, Constance goes in her bedroom and starts snooping through her things. She doesn't know what she will find but hopes Mae has something she can take to a pawn shop and exchange for cash. Being careful to leave everything as she finds it, she goes through all four dresser drawers. There is nothing in them except clothes. She looks several other places around the room and finds nothing.

Now frustrated, she looks in Mae's closet. She searches through pockets of clothing and kneels to check her shoe boxes. There is nothing valuable in any of them. She sits on the floor, looking around, and curses. She starts to leave the room and notices a small drawer on Mae's nightstand. She opens it and sees a picture of a man, a wedding band, and a box of unused checks. Constance opens the box of checks and looks at the starting number on each book. The last book in the box starts with number 1901. She pulls it out and makes sure to place everything back as she found it. She leaves Mae's room, walks to the living room, and picks up the photo album Mae showed her, the one with letters Mae wrote to June that were returned undeliverable. She takes a letter and envelope to work with her. At work, she practices writing Mae's signature until she feels confident it is a good match. Within a couple of days, she has a fake ID made and starts writing checks for cash.

The next week, Mae walks in her front door, looking distressed. Her hair is stuck to her forehead from the three o'clock heat wave of the summer days. She yells, "Constance, we need to talk," as she pulls her hair from her forehead and wraps it around each ear.

Constance walks into the living room, where Mae is setting her purse on a table and taking a seat on a long sofa. Constance stands in the living room doorway.

"Okay," she says. "What's goin' on?"

Mae looks at Constance and says, "I had a meeting with my bank today. Someone has been using one of my checkbooks. Now I have no money in my account."

Constance quickly moves next to Mae on the sofa. In a high-pitched, amazed-sounding voice, she says, "What?"

"Yes," Mae says. "Worse than that, all the checks I wrote for my bills this month have bounced."

Constance stands up and starts pacing. "Oh my God. No!"

"Constance, have you had anyone in my house?" Mae asks.

Constance sits back down and says, "Yes, ma'am. A few people I met at church. They were only in the front room. Some of them went to the bathroom down the"—she slows her speech—"hallllllllll. You think one of them slipped in your room and—"

Mae cuts her off and says, "Anything is possible, even with church folks."

Constance touches her cheeks with her hands and says, "Oh, Cousin Mae, I'm sorry. I swear. I can't believe they would do this. I'm so grateful to God to be here. I'm learning so much about God's love. What can I do?"

Mae looks at her for a moment and then says, "You can start by giving me the names of everyone you've had in my home and when."

"It was just one time," Constance says quickly.

"I need a list to give to the police," Mae says.

Constance says, "Okay. I'll write down all their names, every last one of them. I just can't believe they would do this. I'm so sorry."

Mae looks sick and dazed. She stares down at the floor and says slowly, "Here I am trying to help you; now I need help." Then she looks up at Constance.

Constance stands up and starts to pace again.

"I feel so bad," Constance says. "I don't have any idea who did this."

"Neither do I," Mae says with a sense of resolve, "but I will find out. I serve the true and living God. No devil in hell is going destroy me. I need that list."

Constance sits next to Mae once more and looks Mae in the eyes. "I'm so grateful to God for you," she says.

Mae replies, "We're family; we help each other." Then she drops her head as she shakes it side to side.

Constance tells her, "This is my fault. I'm gonna go and start packing."

Mae lifts her head and says, "I'm not blaming you. You don't have to do that."

"Yes, I do," she says. "I'll be okay. When I get settled, I'll send you some money as soon as I can."

She gives Constance a stern look and says, "Where are you going? Back to your mother?"

"No. I have friends; I can stay with them and they can help me get a job at a factory. I didn't wanna work there, but it's good pay. I'll be fine. Plus I can send you money."

"Get your life together. Stay with God," Mae warns her.

"Oh I will; I swear. And as soon as I can, I'll send you some money."

Constance takes Mae's hands and quickly prays, *"God, please help Cousin Mae. I'm so sorry this happened; please help me make this right. Amen."*

When she finishes her prayer, she walks to her room, sits on the bed, and stares at the wall, thinking about her next move. She feels bad (but not bad enough to tell the Mae truth).

She takes out her little black book and flips through the pages until she sees the name Mrs. Wilts. She notices that there is no first name or address, just a phone number. Constance sighs, thinking, *I know my momma hate my daddy and his momma, and don't want me to know them, but she coulda least had their address.* She sits for a moment, wondering about her father's mother. After a while, she decides to call her when she goes to work.

She makes her way to the phone booth outside the convenience store. A woman inside is sitting on the little seat, holding the phone to her ear with her head down. Constance paces back and forth, looking at the lady impatiently. After a few minutes, she knocks on the phone booth door. The lady looks up at her with red eyes and tears streaming down her cheeks. Constance says through the door, "This is a life emergency."

Still looking at her, the lady says into the phone, "I'll call you back," and then hangs up and opens the door.

Constance rushes in past her and quickly closes the door. She never looks at the lady. She sits down, opens the black book, and finds Mrs. Wilts' number.

While dialing the phone number, Constance thinks about the fact that she has never even met her father, and she's never spoken with his mother. She is hoping that her grandmother is glad to finally hear from her.

When an old woman answers, Constance asks, "Is this the correct number for Mrs. Wilts?"

"Yes."

"May I speak with her please?"

"Who's calling?" the lady asks.

Constance is silent for a moment. Her heart is pounding, and she's nervous.

She swallows and says, "I think ... if she has a granddaughter named Constance Wilts who was born in 1966, I'm her granddaughter."

After she finishes speaking, it seems to her the phone is silent forever. Nervous and determined, Constance holds the phone, waiting for a response.

The old lady says, "I have a granddaughter born in 1966."

Constance smiles a big smile and says, "Grandma!"

The lady becomes deathly silent again.

"Hello?" Constance says. She thinks the old lady has hung up, because she cannot even hear her breathing.

Finally, the old lady says, "What's your daddy's name?"

Constance gets a knot in her throat and forces herself to speak. "I don't know," she says. "I've neva met him. I don't even have a picture. My momma's name is June."

"You are my granddaughter," the old lady says.

"I've waited all my life to meet you," she says to her grandmother. "I'm hoping you will let me come and spend some time with you."

In an exaggerated story, Constance tells her grandmother that she and her mother had a fight, and she left home late one night and sat at the bus station with a little black address book, waiting for morning so she could call her cousin Mae and ask to come for a visit. Her grandma listens as Constance takes shallow breaths and continues to spill her guts about traveling to Mae's house and about how she was blessed to move in with Mae. But now a terrible thing had happened, and she could no longer live with Mae.

"What's the terrible thing?" her grandma asks.

Constance takes a deep breath and tells her version of the story. She explains that Mae's checkbook was stolen; they were not sure by whom, but she and Mae felt it had to be one of the church members she invited into Mae's home for a fellowship brunch. She adds to the aggrandized version of the theft, saying that Mae was going to have to move in with her sister and rent out her home; she ended by saying she felt bad and did not want to be a burden to Mae. "I don't want to go home. I need a place to stay until I can get on my feet," she says, becoming silent.

Grandma remains silent for a while too. Constance breaks the silence and says, "I'm sorry I'm calling you with my problems."

Grandma replies, "This phone call is an answered prayer, but I don't like what I'm hearing. Over twenty years has passed since I laid eyes on you. I had a shouting match with your mother. You were just a newborn; she had you out among people with your head unwrapped and exposed to germs. You brought back twenty years of drama like it was just yesterday. Of course you can come."

Constance thanks her grandmother profusely and gets directions to her home in Charleston, South Carolina, from the bus station before she disconnects the call.

She quickly makes her way back to Mae's home. It is now five o'clock. She knows Mae goes to bed early on Friday nights (and lays in bed reading), which works out perfectly for her because she does not want to discuss the stolen checkbook or list of names. She just wants to leave as quickly as possible. She quietly opens the front door and walks down the hall to her bedroom. She quietly packs her belongings, calls for a taxi, and rolls her luggage bag out to Mae's front porch to wait for the taxi to arrive.

Chapter 3
A Grandmother's Love

When Mae awakes early on Saturday morning, Constance is gone. She finds
a sheet of paper on her kitchen table with a list of names. Mae walks to her
second guest room, which she used primarily as a storage room. She keeps the
closet door locked, because she has a safe in it that contains all of her important
papers, including her box of checkbooks—new and used ones. She only keeps
the box of checks she is currently using in her bedroom. As she unlocks the
closet door, her mind goes back to her conversation with Constance, when
Constance suggested that someone had slipped into her bedroom and stole her
checkbook.

When Mae realizes that Constance would have had to know that her
checkbook was in her room, she becomes furious.

As Constance rides another bus, this time to meet her grandmother,
Constantine Wilts sits at her kitchen table, sipping at a cup of green
tea, thinking about how she has always wanted a relationship with her
granddaughter. Constance's father is her only child, and Constance is her only
grandchild. She sips her tea and thinks about how she cannot believe how evil
June is. She believed that God would make this day come. And she knew that
one day she would have a relationship with her granddaughter when she was
older, and at that time she would explain why she had not been in her life.

She continues sipping her tea and thinks about calling her son. She decides
it would be better to wait. She thinks back to what he went through with June.

*   *   *

As the bus rolls up 95 northbound, Constance reclines her seat, places both hands behind her head, and lifts her chin into the air with attitude. She smiles confidently, knowing that she was right in betting that her father's mother would be glad to hear from her. Most of all, she is happy that she does not have to go back to her mother.

She thinks about her mother and says to herself, *Get your own rent; you're good at it.* Her thoughts change to her feelings for her father. She has serious issues with him not being in her life. The thought almost makes her change her mind about visiting his mother, yet she is desperate and needs to get far away from Mae. This seemed to be the perfect time to get acquainted with Grandma Wilts. Constance sensed from the telephone call that her grandma was a sharp thinker and no-nonsense woman, but she is confident she can stay with her until she plans her next destination.

At seven in the morning, the bus rolls into North Charleston, South Carolina. When the bus comes to a stop, Constance steps off and looks up at the sky. The humid weather outside replaces the chill from the bus's air-conditioner. She sees a couple of motels, a gas station, and several mom-and-pop stores. She notices the ladies of the evening, walking back and forth in skimpy outfits and high heels.

As she stares at them, she is startled by a male's voice from behind her saying, "I got the latest brand names in purses, dirt cheap."

She jumps as she turns around. "No thank you," she says quickly, as the man walks past her.

The environment makes her nervous. She shakes it off and enters the station and uses the station's phone to call a taxi. After thirty minutes, a taxi pulls up and stops in front of the station. She walks to the back door and gets in, telling the driver where to go. The taxi driver gets her to Grandma's house in fifteen minutes. Grandma has a big, two-story house with a wraparound porch. Constance is surprised to see such a big house. She pays the taxi driver and walks up the steep steps to the porch and uses the knocker.

Grandma Wilts opens the door. Constance lays eyes on a tall woman with an authoritative look about her.

"Well, just look atcha," Grandma Wilts says. "I haven't seen you since you were knee-high to a grasshopper. You look just like your daddy."

Constance smiles until she hears the last words her grandma says. She frowns.

"With all due respect, Grandma, he's a father, not a daddy."

Without taking a breath, Grandma says, "Yes, he is, and a damn good one too! I raised my son to be a man. He was young and didn't know what he was gettin' into. He was a young man in school, getting his education. When he found out how that woman lived her life, he wanted nothin' more than to take you from her and outta that lifestyle. A-many-a-nights, I cried and prayed with him on the phone, because that woman took you, his newborn baby, and moved, and no one, not even her own mother, knew where you were or if you were okay. Prayer is the only reason my son didn't lose his mind. And we togetha prayed, and God told us to rest assured that this day would come."

She calms down and then continues, "There was no way he could stay with that woman. You of all people should know that. You here. Now, this is no way for us to start off. Come on in. Let's get to know each other."

Constance does not say a word and wonders if she should stay or go. She steps through the doorway and follows her grandmother to a large room filled with antique furniture. Constance sees a picture of a beautiful young woman who looks a lot like her.

"Is that your daughta?" she asks her grandma.

"She looks a lot like you, huh?" Grandma smiles. Still looking at the picture, Constance nods her head in agreement. Grandma says, "Child, that's me when I was 'bout your age—one of my best pictures." Grandma Wilts looks at her and smiles. "First time I laid eyes on you, I knew you were my twin, even as a newborn."

Constance smiles and walks closer to the picture. She sees the name Constantine and looks back at her grandma, who walks up to the picture. They both smile and give each other a big hug. Grandma Wilts kisses her on the head and explains, "We decided to shorten your name from mine."

"We?" Constance says.

"When I came to New Orleans for your birth, your mom and I started out okay. Huh; I didn't know her and she didn't know me."

"Thanks, Grandma, for lettin' me come," Constance says. "I feel so bad 'bout what happened to Cousin Mae."

Grandma, who was not familiar with June's side of the family, asks, "How are y'all kin?"

"She my mother's first cousin," Constance says. "She's sweet. I really love her. She lives for Jesus. That's why I went there. I knew she would be an inspiration for me."

Grandma places her right hand on her hip and broadens her shoulders. "This story you told me on the phone, the Spirit is tellin' me there is more to it than you told."

"No ma'am," Constance says in an innocent, childlike voice. "I really hate that somebody stole her money."

"Well, you're here now and you're welcome to stay but you gon have to work. Did you work anywhere when you stayed with Mae? You can't stay here for free."

Constance looks up and says, "I know, Grandma. I don't expect to."

Grandma stares back at Constance and says, "You not—expectin' or not."

There is a bit of silence as Constance gathers her thoughts. She knows Grandma is not the one to sass.

"I already have a job interview lined up," she says.

Shocked, Grandma widens her eyes and says, "A job interview? Child, it's Saturday and you just got here. How you gotta job lined up?"

Constance puts a big smile on her face; practicing her skills of deceit, she says, "Grandma, you know God works in mysterious ways. I met someone at the bus station. They were waiting for someone to arrive, and I overheard them saying they owned a business. I interrupted and said I was new in town and needed a job. We talked 'bout my skills, and they asked me to come see 'em on Monday. God is good, Grandma. God is good."

Grandma looks at Constance suspiciously and says slowly, "Yes, he is. What's this person's name? What kind of business is it, and where is it?"

Wanting time to get her lies together, Constance quickly says, "I promise I'll tell you all about it. It's that time of the month for me, and I don't feel well. May I please lay down for a while?"

Grandma stares at Constance and then says, "Sure. Your bedroom is down the hall; are you hungry? Want something to drink?"

"No, Grandma; thank you, but not right now," Constance replies while touching her stomach. Grandma walks her down the hallway, and Constance follows, rolling her luggage bag behind her.

She walks Constance to her room; standing in the doorway, she says, "Thank God you are not pregnant. And don't get that way either. I don't allow strangers in my house, period. Understand?"

Grandma walks into the guest room and over to the bed. She picks up two small decorative pillows and holds them in her arms. Constance enters behind her, looks around the room, and says, "Wow." She looks at a queen-size bed with a cream-colored chiffon valance over the top of it that hangs down to the floor. The chest of drawers, night stand, and dresser match the bed. The bedspread and pillowcases have beautiful green and yellow flowers on a cream background that matches the valance. The walls are light green with yellow face boards all around them at the top and bottom. The room is warm, cozy, and very inviting. She says, "This is so beautiful."

Grandma replies, "We knew you would like it."

"This is for me?" Constance eyes widen as she looks at Grandma.

"I've changed it out over the years. There used to be a crib in that corner," she says, pointing to the space on the left side of the bed. Your dad and I fixed it up for you when you were first born. We thought you would be given to us, and we wanted you to have a room fit for a queen." Grandma stops speaking and looks down.

There is a picture on the wall of a handsome young man with a big smile on his face. Constance walks over to the picture; she looks back at Grandma and says, "This is my father?" Grandma nods. "How old was he here?"

"Not much older than you," says Grandma as she walks over and stands next to Constance.

"What's his name?" Constance asks.

"Carlton," Grandma replies.

"Does he live here?" Constance asks.

"No," Grandma responds quickly. Constance was about to ask another question but Grandma cuts her off, saying, "We have a lot of catching up to do. But for now, back to what I was saying ..."

"Yes, ma'am," Constance says. "I understand you don't allow strangers in your house; I'm not pregnant and I'm not gonna get that way. I don't even have a boyfriend. I'm not interested in anyone but Jesus. I want to live for God and serve him only."

Looking Constance directly in the eyes, Grandma says, "Okay. Just don't bring any of your 'live for God' people in my house. Ever. Do I make myself clear?"

"Yes, ma'am. I swear I won't."

Grandma steps closer to Constance and says, "Swearing is for fools. Just don't do it."

"Yes, ma'am," Constance says softly.

Grandma leaves the room. Constance looks around again and says, "All this, just for me."

She lays across the bed and thinks about her father and how she wishes he would have been in her life. Her mind quickly drifts to Mae, but she does not allow herself to think about what she did to her cousin. Instead she wonders what's going on with Jim and her mother. She returns to thinking about Grandma and how she can continue the lie about already having a job. She closes her eyes real tight and decides she will not think at all. The silence of the room, along with the comfort of the bed, is relaxing. She listens to the clock ticking on the dresser across from the bed; the last times she looks at it, it show nine o'clock a.m. She falls asleep.

At five o'clock, she awakes and makes her way to the bathroom across from her bedroom. Once she freshens up, she walks down the hall to the living room and finds Grandma watching TV. Grandma looks up at her and says, "Are you rested now?"

"Yes ma'am," she replies.

"I made supper. You like beef stew and rice?"

"Yes," Constance says, as she follows Grandma to the kitchen.

Grandma fixes them both a plate and places them on the kitchen table. They sit; Grandma blesses the food, and they eat. While they eat, Grandma asks Constance, "Where is your home?"

"Suffolk, Virginia."

"Y'all got family there?"

"No ma'am. Just me, Mama, and Jim."

"Jim? That's your brother?"

"Yes."

"How old?"

"Ten."

Grandma says slowly, "Suffolk. You been there all these years?"

"No ma'am; we lived in Philadelphia, Azalea Acres, Saratoga, Lenox, Lakeview Heights, Riverview, Eastover, and West Jericho. They're all in Virginia. But we've been in Suffolk the longest."

Grandma looks at Constance and says, "How's life been for you?"

Constance shrugs her shoulders; her eyes instantly water.

"Child, what's wrong?"

"A lot. I thought I was rested but I feel tired again."

"Once you finish eating, you lay back down. Your body needs rest, child; that's why you feel so tired," Grandma says.

Constance finishes eating and walks back to the room. Grandma looks in on her a little later and sees her sleeping peacefully. She enters the room, closes the curtains, and quietly leaves the room, closing the door behind her.

The next morning at seven o'clock, Grandma looks in the room and notices Constance is still sleeping; she walks over and opens the curtains. "Do you always sleep this much?" she asks in a loud enough voice to wake Constance.

Constance opens her eyes, looks out the window at the beautiful morning, and notices Grandma has on a house robe and pajamas.

"I can't believe I slept through the whole evening," she says.

Grandma replies, "You did; I checked in on you at six. You were out cold. Sunday service starts in three hours, so we don't have much time."

"It won't take me long," Constance replies as she gets out of bed and walks over to her luggage bag.

By 8:30, Constance joins Grandma in the kitchen for breakfast. Grandma notices Constance has on a long summer dress with quarter sleeves and a round neck. "I like your taste in clothing," Grandma tells Constance. "That dress is very appropriate for a young lady to wear to church."

"Thank you," Constance replies.

She decides not to say anything else. She does not want to say something she thinks is okay, but it upsets Grandma. They finish their breakfast and walk out the side door to the carport. As they get in Grandma's Buick Electra, Constance asks, "How long is the service?"

"About two hours," Grandma replies as she turns onto the street. They travel across the Cooper River Bridge, approximately fifteen miles to a small white church. They enter. The church has colorful stained glass windows and old wooden benches and floors. They take a seat at the front. Constance thinks about her church attendance with Mae and how she did not want to start that up again.

At the end of the service, the preacher asks if anyone has a prayer request. Grandma stands and says, "God has blessed me this day. I am sitting here with my granddaughter that I have not seen for over twenty years." She looks down, places her hand on Constance's shoulder, and then looks up at the congregation, continuing, "God told me this day would come. I believed him and I waited. I knew he would not let me die until I seen this day. She is here and I am well. I thank God we are going to start our grandmother and granddaughter relationship that I have been waiting on for twenty years. And I'm asking for prayers."

As Grandma Wilts sits down, the preacher says, "Mother, we thank God with you, and we will certainly be praying that God will bless you both to have many years to make up for lost time." He continues with a prayer and ends the service.

On the ride home, Grandma and Constance roll down the windows and enjoy the warm breeze. Grandma tells Constance about shopping on King Street, the market area where salves were bought and sold, and the dinner cruises on the Battery. Constance says she was looking forward to seeing all of Charleston. As they drive back to the house, Constance asks Grandma about her husband and the rest of the Wilts family. Grandma tells Constance her grandfather died when Carlton was a little boy, adding that she would meet her father and the rest of the family soon.

As they park the car, Constance thinks Grandma's response was a little strange. She walks slowly behind Grandma as they enter the house. Constance feels that something is just not right. This was a familiar feeling for her. She remembered it from when she was five years old and her mother woke her in the middle of the night to tell her they had to move immediately. She asked her mom if everything was all right, and she had replied yes. But the truth was that everything was not all right. June was running from her landlord and others she had borrowed and stolen money from. Constance knows this feeling very well, and she has had it often throughout her life.

She thinks about how she has never been wrong when she's had it. She thought to herself, *There is something Grandma is not saying, but what?*

Grandma quickly changes clothing and warms their meal. After they eat, Grandma goes into the living room and pulls out a large photo album stuffed with pictures. She calls to Constance. Constance walks out of the kitchen into the living room. Grandma is sitting on her couch with the photo album in her lap. She asks Constance to come and sit by her. Constance takes a seat next to her, and Grandma opens the photo album and lays half of it on Constance's lap. She shows Constance all the family members, making sure to mention their ages and when they passed if they are deceased.

Constance looks at the pictures and listens attentively to every word Grandma speaks. As Grandma flips the pages, she tells Constance about the ones she felt were most significant: "This is your granddad, Carlton Senior. We still own this land near the church and this rental property here in town. These two men are your great-uncles; they were skillful in tailoring. This one is your second cousin; he was a mechanic; he's retired now. These two are blacksmiths; they live in New York now. And this one, he's the family scholar, our Harvard grad." She closes the photo album and looks at Constance. "We are a family of proud, hard-working people. Your dad was the last baby to be born into our aging family. He has no siblings because when Carlton Senior died, your dad was five years old; I lost my desire for having more kids, and marriage too. I put all my energy into your dad; maybe too much. I blame myself for him dating your mother."

Constance asks, "What did Granddad die from?"

Grandma looks at her and says, "Double pneumonia. Both of his lungs collapsed." Grandma was silent for a moment. She just looks at Constance and then says, "I know he'll never admit it, but I think dating your mom was the way he chose to rid himself of the nice guy reputation. He wanted to show his college friends he could be tough by dating a wild girl."

Constance looks confused.

Grandma continues, "When I sent him to college in New Orleans, I expected he would date someone at his school, but not a street woman." Constance takes a deep breath. Grandma quickly says, "I know this is hard for you to hear, but you have got to know the truth. Since Carlton was a little boy, he was always considered the nice guy. That reputation followed him from grade school to college. He hated it. I think your mother was not his type, but she was just what he thought he needed for his new reputation—a tough guy with a wild girl. He didn't know she was a slut."

Constance jumps up and says, "I don't wanna talk anymore."

Grandma pulls her back down on the sofa by her hand. "Sweetie, why are you here?" she asks.

She and Constance look at each other for a long time, in silence. Tears start to roll down Constance's cheek.

Grandma says, "I know your mother. Very well. I tried to get her to change. Everybody did: my son, his friends, and all of your family. The more we tried, the worse she got. Carlton wanted to marry her."

"Did he love her?" Constance asks.

"Say he did," Grandma replies. "I know he loves you."

Constance raises her voice. "How do you know that? Where is he? He hasn't even come to see me."

"You been here less than forty-eight hours and you're judging him because he has not come here to see you, when that woman kept you from him all your life," Grandma replies sharply.

Constance stands up and looks down at Grandma. "You haven't told him I'm here, have you?"

Grandma looks up at her. "No. Did you hear anything I said to you yesterday? My son almost lost his mind. He was raised to be a responsible man. He could not be that for you because he did not know where you were. I will not have him be hurt again. I will let him know, when I know."

"Know what? I'm not a slut like my momma is?" Constance asks.

"Yes," Grandma answers, looking Constance directly in her eyes. "I'm glad you're here. But I will protect my son. The two of you have my blood running through your veins. Just trust me."

Constance does not reply. She leaves the living room, goes to her room, and lays down. After her nap, she opens her bedroom door. She can hear the TV in the living room and figures Grandma is in there. She walks to the living room to join her. When Grandma looks up and sees Constance, she turns the TV down low and asks, "Would you like to talk? I care about you. I want you to share what you've been through. We don't have to talk about your mother."

"No ma'am, at least not right now," Constance replies.

For the rest of the evening, they laugh while watching TV together. After the local news, they say good night and go to their bedrooms. The next morning, Constance is up bright and early. She remembers she told Grandma she has a job interview. She thinks about their conversation yesterday and is now more eager to prove she is not like her mother. She leaves a note on the kitchen table: "Gone to my interview," and leaves the house while Grandma is still in her bedroom.

Constance never did meet anyone at the bus station. She dresses like she is going to a job interview. She finds the nearest service station and asks the attendant the name of the city's most upscale strip club. Then she asks to use his phone and telephone book. She finds the club in the Yellow Pages, writes down the address, and calls to make sure the place is still open for business. She leaves the service station and takes the bus there. She knows this is the best time to meet the strip club's owner, so she makes her way to the club, hoping to run a con for a sugar daddy or a well-paying job.

The strip club is located in the tourist part of downtown known as the Hot Spot. The owner, Steven, is a muscular, handsome man in his late forties. He is at the club to receive the beverage shipment for the week. Steven gets out of his car just as a beer truck pulls up in front of the club.

Constance is a seductress young lady with classy appeal. When the bus reaches downtown, she exits the bus and starts walking in the direction of the club. From two blocks away, she sees a man outside the club, talking to another man unloading a beer truck. *That must be the owner,* she thinks. Now only a few feet away, she slows her stride and allows her hips to sway.

Constance's sultry voice gets their attention. "Excuse me, sir," Constance says. "Am I near Main Street?"

The man who looks like the owner motions for the other man to take his load of beer into the club. The truck driver stumbles as he attempts to look at Constance and roll the cases of beer on his dolly across the club's front entrance. The man holding the door ignores the stumbling delivery man and stares at Constance.

"Not really." He collects himself and then continues, "Not at all."

Constance shakes her head, turns her back to him, and looks at the buildings around her. Then she turns around and faces him. "Just my luck," she says. She reaches to shake his hand while saying, "Thank you."

He releases the door, reaches out his hand, and says, "What's your name and what's on Main Street?"

"Constance Wilts. A job, I hope."

"Call me Steven," he says as he opens the door again and motions for Constance to enter. "What kind of a job?"

Constance walks into the club ahead of Steven and stands inside the entrance.

"Anything. No, really. Something in the clerical field."

Steven, trying hard not to let it be obvious that he is checking her out, keeps his eyes focused on her face.

"I have a small business besides owning this club," he says. "Maybe you can help me out."

Pretending to be innocent, Constance acts as though she did not hear what he said. "Oh! I can't work here; I just moved here to take care of my grandmother in the evenings. She lives alone and need someone around," she says.

Steven motions for her to follow him to his office. They go into his office. "Where're you from?" he says.

"New York," she replies.

"I understand," he says. "I'm not talking about working here." He picks a business card up off his desk and hands it to her. "I'm talking about here."

Constance reads the card aloud: "Applegate Apartments, Month-to-Month Leasing Available." She looks up at him and says, "Really?"

"Possibly," he says. "What do you think?"

"What's the catch?" she asks.

"No catch," he says. "Just a job. Meet me at the address on the card tomorrow morning at nine o'clock."

"Thanks." She smiles. "You've made my day."

Sizing her up, Steven smiles and says, "You're welcome. You've made mine."

She places his card in her purse and says, "Where are the state office buildings?"

"There are some on Bridgeview Drive," he replies, "but that's North Charleston."

Constance thanks him again and tells him she will see him tomorrow morning and leaves.

Constance makes her way back to Grandma's house. Constance comes in through the front door, hears Grandma in the kitchen, and walks back to see her. Grandma is washing her breakfast dishes. Constance picks up an apple out of the fruit basket on the table and takes a bite.

Grandma turns and looks at her, still washing dishes, and asks, "How'd the interview go?"

"Haven't had it yet. Thought it was today, but he gave me an application and said for me to return tomorrow 'cause somethin' came up." She then takes another bite of the apple.

Grandma stops washing dishes, dries her hands, and walks toward Constance. She asks to see the application.

Constance, thinking Grandma may know this man and know that he owns a strip club, reaches into her purse and whines, "Oh man, I musta left it on his desk when I shook his hand."

Grandma takes a seat at the kitchen table and looks at Constance very suspiciously. "Where is this place?" she asks.

Constance gives Grandma a look of urgency. "May I please call and check on Cousin Mae? I won't stay on the phone long. I feel God is leading me to talk to her." Constance is always able to divert Grandma's attention when she mentions Cousin Mae. Grandma's heart goes out to Mae, and she can't seem to shake the thought of what she has heard about the event.

Shaking her head in pity, Grandma says, "Go ahead. I pray she finds out who's behind this." She stops shaking her head and looks up at Constance with an interrogating look. "Child, you sure you don't know who did this to her?"

"I don't, Grandma. I don't. If I knew, I woulda told the police, but I don't," Constance quickly replies as she retreats to her room.

She picks up the phone on the nightstand next to her bed and pretends to dial a number. After she dials a bogus number, she looks back at the bedroom door to see if Grandma is standing there. When she does not see her, she breathes a sigh of relief and then sits on the bed. She sits and thinks, *Why am I nervous? So what if he owns a strip club. He's a businessman. I just know she'll think I'm working at his club; I can't tell her. I have nowhere to go. I'll just say the job I'm tryin' to get is at the state office.*

After a moment, Constance returns to the kitchen where Grandma is still sitting and says, "Cousin Mae didn't ansa."

Even more suspicious, Grandma says, "Well, if God wanted you two talkin', you would have been talkin'. I don't understand why you would invite someone into her home—a stranger you hadn't known that long—and leave them long enough for them to steal." Shaking her head, Grandma continues, "Uh uh. You know much mo' than you sayin'. Child, are you sure—"

Constance cuts Grandma off by saying, "Let me tell you 'bout the job. It's in the state building on Bridgeview Drive."

"State? Doing what?"

"Answering the phone, Grandma."

Grandma says, "Yeah? But you said this person was a business owner, not a state employee. I don't take kindly to lying, young lady. Now, if you can't get a job, my church needs someone to help with the day care center. You know, cleaning and helping with the kids. You don't have a criminal record, do you?" Grandma thinks about it and then says out loud, "Probably should."

Again Constance ignores Grandma's response, knowing she is not one to sass, and says, "I'm goin' back for my interview tomorrow, Grandma. I promise, if I don't get the job, I'd love to help out in the day care center. Who do I call?"

"I'll get the number," Grandma says.

"Okay," she replies.

Instead of watching TV with Grandma, Constance goes to bed early. She lay in bed thinking about Grandma. She feels Grandma loves her but doesn't trust her; she is glad she's there but does not want to be taken advantage of, like Mae; and she definitely wants to make sure she is not like her mom. Constance feels like she is starting to love Grandma. She looks around her beautiful room and thinks about the house, the land, and the rental property. Her mind goes to thoughts of her dad and the fact that everything Grandma owns should be theirs.

She says to herself, *I can handle Grandma; I know she's glad I'm here; when I own all of this, I'll show Mom just who I am.* Feeling good, she drifts off to sleep. The next morning, she awakes early and leaves the house before Grandma starts stirring.

When Steven hears the front door of his duplex office open, he looks up.

"Well," he says, "I see you're able to handle yourself in a strange city. You got here with no problem?"

"No problem," Constance says, assuring him.

Admiring her beauty, innocence, and cockiness, Steven says, "I own these duplexes from the corner to the end of the road behind this building. I need an assistant to help me screen potential tenants, book repair appointments, and collect rent. I've had several people in this position, but none of them were dependable." He motions her to have a seat across from his desk. "Tell me about yourself."

Constance sits down and says, "As I mentioned yesterday, I'm interested in eight-to-five work so I can be home with my grandmother at night. I can do some typing but I'm not very fast. I've worked convenience stores and fast food restaurants, and other jobs where I've had to type, answer the phone, file, and handle mail. I can do anything," she says.

"Oh really?" he replies.

"Yes," she answers, while smiling and looking directly into his eyes.

"You're pretty confident of yourself," he says, smiling back.

"I'm one of those people that catch on quickly," she says. "Whatever I put my mind to, I can do."

"Okay. Do you have a resume?"

"No," she says, giving him a bigger smile. "I was planning to get a list of job openings from the state office and decide which ones I wanted to apply for. I wasn't expecting to meet you on yesterday."

"Well, I'm glad you did. Tell you what, here's an application. After you fill it out and I check it, the job is yours if you're interested."

Constance takes the application and says, "I am interested. This sounds like the job for me."

"I hope this works out."

"You will not regret this; I want this job."

"I thought you'd feel that way," Steven says. "Anyone who moves to a new city and puts their life on hold to help their grandmother is someone I don't mind taking a chance on."

Constance smiles and says, "Well, thank you."

"You look okay, but you know I have to check you out first," Steven says. "Do you have a criminal record? You're not running from the law in another city, are you?"

"That's beneath me," Constance replies sharply. "I am sold out to God. I love him so. He is my all and all. And I'm his child. I'm a sheep of his pasture; I know his voice and I only follow him." She calms herself and looks at Steven. "No, I am not running from the law. I'm sorry for going off like that. I just can't imagine being anything less than a representative of Christ. Do I still have the job?"

"Yes, you do," says Steven, "You can start tomorrow morning at nine o'clock. We'll see how it works out."

"Thank you so much," Constance says. "I'll be here."

She turns and makes her way to the door. When she reaches the door, she looks back at Steven and says, "God bless you."

"He just did," Steven says. After Constance leaves, Steven's phone rings. She stands outside his door and listens as he says, "Not another problem! I'll have to get to it later. Later; I'm on my way across town, my new club opens tonight." He slams the phone down.

Constance makes her way back to Grandma's house. She opens the front door and yells, "I got the job!" with excitement. She walks through several rooms until she finds Grandma in the den, sitting quietly, reading her Bible. Constance stands in the den's doorway.

"I start tomorrow. I prayed last night, this morning, and while I was waiting for the interview. I believed in my heart, and God answered my prayer."

"Great," Grandma says. "Well, here"—Grandma hands Constance the number for the person at the church day care center—"Keep this number, just in case God changes his mind 'bout your new job, 'cause you will certainly need another one."

Constance tells Grandma that she has already figured out the bus route she needs to take and bought herself a bus pass. Grandma smiles at her and nods her head in approval as she listens to Constance go on and on about her new job and how she is already starting to love the city.

Living with Grandma and working with Steven is financially great for Constance. Although Grandma insisted Constance have a job, she does not ask her to pay for anything. Grandma visits her attorney to discuss adding Constance to her will. Afterward she makes her way to a tailor and gives him instructions to make a dress for her granddaughter, saying she's planning a formal event.

Financially, Constance is doing great. She still has most of Mae's money and all of her pay from working with Steven. Her problem is Grandma, who won't let her have friends over or go out at night. She doesn't even use the phone except to ask to call Mae, which she never does. She makes sure she goes to church with Grandma every Sunday.

I like Grandma, she thinks to herself, *but this is not the life I wanna live.*

After two months, she has had all she can take and is ready to make her move. Two months to the day after she arrived in Charleston, she sits down and plans her next move.

On the following Monday morning, she arrives at the duplex office, looking sad and sounding as though her world has crumbled. Steven is going through papers on his desk. She says slowly, "Good morning, Steven," as she walks to her desk.

Steven looks up from his stack of papers and says, "Who died on you last night?"

Pretending to cry as she flops down at her desk, Constance says, "My grandmother."

Steven stands up quickly, walks over to her, and says, "Oh, Constance, I'm so sorry. What are you doing here? How can I help?"

Constance pretends to hold back tears and collect herself.

"My family is very private. I shouldn't say anything, but we can't afford to bury her. And I need to get her back to New York." Her eyes tear up and she drops her head.

"How much do you need?" Steven asks.

Constance flails her hands and says, "Steven, I can't pay you back. I don't even know if Grandma's house is paid for. I may not be able to stay in it anymore."

Steven leans down, reaches out with both hands, gently grabs each of her shoulders, and turns her toward him in her chair.

He asks earnestly, "How much do you need?"

Constance looks him in the eye and says, "Honestly, whatever you can give." Her tears are now rolling down her cheeks as she shrugs her shoulders and shakes her head.

Totally taken by her con and still holding her shoulders, Steven says, "You didn't have to come in today. You could have just called. I certainly would have understood." He releases her shoulders, stands up, and takes a deep breath. "What are your plans for getting her back to New York?"

Constance looks up at Steven. "We're trying to get what we need so I can bring her back this Wednesday."

Steven looks at Constance for a moment. Then he says, "Before you leave on Wednesday, I'll have something for you. Come on, I'll drive you home."

Constance quickly stands up and says, "Oh no! I'm not going back there. Thanks, but I really want to be alone and spend some time with God."

She walks to the door, looks back at Steven as the tears roll down her cheeks, and then closes it behind her.

Steven arrives at the office on Wednesday morning and sees Constance working at her desk.

"Constance, I'll take care of this stuff," he says.

"I just need to do something," she says.

She looks at him with puffy red eyes. He reaches in his pocket and hands her a cashier's check for $2,500 and additional cash to purchase her plane ticket to New York.

"Are you gonna be all right?" he asks.

She stands up, looks him in the eyes, and says, "God is my strength."

He hugs her and then kisses her forehead.

Constance looks at him and says, "I really like this city. I don't want to go back to New York. But don't worry, God as my witness, I'll pay this back," holding up the money he gave her.

Steven smiles at her and kisses her forehead again. He places his arms around her shoulders, holding her tightly. For a long while he does not let go. When he finally releases her, he walks away from her for a moment.

He walks back to her and says, "I think I know you as well as you know yourself. I figured you had grown fond of this city. When you get back, I will have one of the apartments all fixed up for you. You take all the time you need to pay me back. I appreciate the job you've done here. It's taken such a load off me."

Constance grips the money behind her back and looks at him with an innocent smile.

"Thanks. I do want to come back. I feel this is the place for me—away from family and their problems." Steven smiles in agreement. She continues, "I would love to stay in one of the apartments. I expect to pay rent, so I'll get a second job."

"You'll do no such thing," Steven says quickly. "We'll work all that out later." Steven watches Constance walk to the door. "Let me drive you home," he says.

"I need to be alone," Constance says. "Really, I am okay. I'll call you." She touches the doorknob.

"Do you need help with your grandmother's house?" Steven asks. "I have connections. You don't have to live in it, but you might be able to rent it out."

With humble charm, she says, "No, thank you. My family will handle the house business. They're very private. When I return, I want to start classes to get licensed as a property manager. I want to learn from you how to get my own duplexes. I'll call you." She gives him a warm smile.

He says nothing but smiles back. She opens the door and leaves.

As she walks away, she is smiling inside and out. She thinks to herself, *I'm good, real good.* She knows he wants her really badly. She looks at her watch and sees it is 9:45. She makes her way to the bus stop and takes a bus back to her grandma's house. She is surprised and happy that Grandma is not home.

First, she calls for a taxi. Then she packs half of her clothes and leaves the rest neatly arranged in her closet.

She leaves her grandma a note that says, "I'm going to check on Cousin Mae. I'll be back. Love, Constance."

The taxi driver blows the horn, and she lays the pen and Grandma's house keys next to the note on the kitchen table. Then she turns the door knob to the locked position and closes the door behind her.

"Airport please," was all she says. As the taxi driver pulls away from Grandma's house, he looks in his rear view mirror and notices she's reading a book. She looks up at him and then holds the book up higher to hide her face, hoping he remains quiet. It works, the driver takes her to the airport and does not say anything to her the entire trip. They reach the airport; she pays him and exits the taxi with her luggage bag.

Chapter 4
Conning and Running

The airport entrance is crowded and noisy with people rushing in the automatic doors. She quickly rolls her luggage bag in through the doors and barely escapes hitting a young child standing with his parent's right inside the entrance. After apologizing to the parents and child, she slows her pace and sits on a bench in the ticket area. She pulls out the black address book and searches for another one of her relatives to visit. She flips almost to the last page of the address book and sees her Aunt Vivian's name. To her delight there is a number and address for Vivian's daughter, AJ, listed right below Vivian's information.

She looks at the number and thinks to herself, *If Mom doesn't want to be bothered with anyone in her family, why does she bother to keep their numbers?* "Thanks, Mom," she says as she looks around for a telephone booth. She sees one about five feet away from her bench. She walks over, positions her body so she can see her luggage bag, and calls the number.

AJ answers on the first ring. Constance says, "This is your first cousin Constance. I know we have not talked in years, but I was hoping to come for a visit. Do you mind?"

AJ says, "Constance? Now this has to be God's providence. I was just speaking with my mom about you last weekend. How've you been? Where are you?"

Constance says, "Right now I'm in the Charleston airport waiting to get a ticket, if you feel up for company."

AJ replies, "Don't be silly; of course I want to see you. Charleston? Who do you know there?"

"My father's mother lives here. I've been here with her since I moved out from Mom," Constance replies.

AJ is speechless for a moment and then says, "Okay. I have a million questions, but they can wait until you get here."

Constance looks up with a big smile and says, "Thank you so much; is your address still 555 Lonestar Avenue, Atlanta?"

AJ says, "Yes; how did you know?"

"Mom has it in her address book. I'll call you when I get to Atlanta," Constance says. She thanks AJ and then hangs up the phone. She walks to the ticket counter and purchases a one-way ticket to Atlanta. She feels good about going to Georgia, because she's betting AJ has not spoken to Mae, and she is confident that Mae, Grandma Wilts, and Steven do not know each other, so they have no way of determining her whereabouts.

While she waits for her plane, she finds a restaurant and eats lunch, browses several of the shops, and then makes her way back to the boarding area. She thinks about calling her mother but decides against it, reminding herself that she is mad at her. She watches people come and go, focusing on those dressed in business attire, and tries to listen to their conversations. She sees a couple of sophisticated-looking businesswomen carrying briefcases.

One of the ladies sits next to her. Constance looks at the cover of the magazine she is holding; the title is *Successful Woman.* Soon a man walks up and kisses the lady on the cheek. The lady stands up, and she and the man smile and hug each other. They walk away. She notices the man never looks at the woman's body, although she is very sexy; he only looks at the woman's face.

When they are out of sight, Constance walks over to the souvenir shop and buys a copy of *Successful Woman.* She reads it from cover to cover while waiting to depart.

As she finishes reading the magazine, the intercom announces, "Delta flight 886 to Atlanta, Georgia, is now boarding zones one through four." She stands up and gets in line.

After the plane takes off, she reclines her seat and closes her eyes. She rehearses in her mind what she needs to say to get AJ to let her stay with her.

She wants nothing more than to have an education and a career and to be in a loving relationship. She tells herself, *The games are over; things are going to be different. No more lying, using people, or stealing.* To make herself feel good, she tells herself that the things she did and said to Mae, Grandma Wilts, and Steven were her mother's fault, because of how she was raised. She decides she will pretend the three of them do not exist so she does not have to think about them.

Her thoughts return to AJ and how she can get her cousin to help her.

The plane ride is comforting. Constance sits next to the window, staring at the sky, thinking, *I just know she can help me.*

*　*　*

After hanging up the phone with Constance, AJ checks on her guest room to make sure it is tidy. From her guest room, she walks to her foyer and sits in her Mourenx accent chair, next to her birchwood Napoleon telephone stand. She picks up the phone and calls her mother in Savannah, Georgia. When her mother answers, AJ says, "Mom, you will never guess who I just talked to on the phone."

Her mother asks who.

She replies, "Constance." AJ repeats, "Yes," three times while laughing at her mother's surprise. She continues, "She has to be what? About twenty-two now?"

"Yes," Vivian says.

"She says she wants to come here. I told her sure. She's coming from her grandmother's in Charleston."

"Today?"

"She said she was calling from the airport to make sure it was okay."

"I wonder how she find out her grandmother was in Charleston."

"Don't know; maybe Auntie June told her."

"No way; June wouldn't tell her. She must not know where Constance is."

"Why do you say that?"

"I know my sister; she has spent her adult life in hiding with her kids."

"People can change, Ma."

"True, some people, but she hasn't. Constance found her grandmother without June's help."

"Well, I'm glad she's coming."

"Did she say what time her flight gets in?"

"No. She hung up so fast, I didn't get to ask. She said she'll call me from the airport. I'll make sure we come to see you while she's here."

"Okay, honey. You be careful; she has been through a lot," Vivian warns.

"I'll be fine. Love you," AJ says as she hangs up the phone.

She goes to bed that night remembering the family Sunday dinners when her mother would tell them June called and said she and the kids were okay.

Around noon the next day, a taxi drives Constance up to a beautiful mansion. Constance smiles, looking at the house, as the taxi comes to a stop.

AJ hears her doorbell from the family room, where she is sitting quietly. She walks through her foyer to the large front door and opens it. Constance sees her cousin AJ, an attractive young woman of medium height with a petite body.

"Well, hello cousin," AJ says with a big smile on her face. "How are you?"

Constance walks in, places her luggage bag on the floor, and gives AJ a hug.

"I really don't know. God is my strength," she says.

AJ stops hugging Constance and stretches out her arms, still holding Constance's shoulders.

"I'm glad you called," she says. "You surprised me; I didn't know Auntie had my number. So what's going on?"

AJ walks Constance from her foyer, down the long hallway. Constance looks at all the pictures hanging along the hallway: AJ in her Marines uniform; AJ in her wedding dress, standing with a handsome man; and several pictures of three kids and a family portrait. They walk into the family room.

"You know how, when you're living for Jesus, everything goes wrong?" Constance says. "That's what's going on with me. But I don't care what happens, I'm stayin' with God. He's my all and all."

The family room is large. On the right side of the room there is a cream and navy loveseat with a gold tree lamp behind it. There is a cream-colored sofa in the center of the room with a marble coffee table in front of it. Positioned on the left side of the room are two navy swivel rocker chairs with a small marble telephone stand in between them. The room has a high ceiling with four strands of lights positioned to light up each area of the room. Two extra large ferns sit atop plant stands, one near the room entrance and the other near a bay window.

Constance stands in the doorway for a moment, just looking. "This is beautiful," she says.

Motioning for Constance to have a seat in one of the rockers, AJ says, "Thank you. I call it my Eden. I come here to unwind."

"I need that; I can't unwind," says Constance.

"Can't or won't?" asks AJ.

"Can't. My life is terrible. Tryin' to be a Christian hasn't helped."

"Yes, I do know the life of a Christian is not easy. I have the battle scars to prove it. But it's worth it." They both look at each other. "I told Mom you were coming for a visit. You said you were with your father's mother?" AJ asks.

Constance answers, "Yes. Grandma was nice. I enjoyed her. She told me things about my dad I didn't know."

"Like what?" AJ asks.

Constance turns her face and, with a far-off look in her eyes, says, "He loves me." She takes a deep breath, looks back at AJ, and continues, "At least one parent loves me."

AJ is silent for a moment. She almost feels guilty for having two normal, loving parents.

"God and all your family love you too," she says.

"Yeah," Constance says, "you're right. I just don't understand why my life is the way it is. I can't explain it."

AJ says, "And you never will. We walk by faith. His word says he loves us and will never leave us nor forsake us; you should always believe that." AJ smiles at Constance and continues, "Your mom loves you too."

"We had an argument, and I left. I haven't talked to her since."

AJ says, "I'm sure Auntie June is worried about you."

Constance quickly replies, "Oh, I'm sure she's worried, but not about me. Our last fight was about her using to me to get rent money."

"From where?" AJ asks.

"Where do you think?" Constance asks, and then she quickly drops her head. She knows she has AJ right where she wants her.

She rubs the back of her neck as if to relieve herself of stress.

"I don't know," she says. "Maybe she's worried. She shouldn't be. God is my strength. I love the Lord, and by serving him, all things work together for my good." She smiles at AJ and folds her arms.

"Exactly," AJ says, then continues, "I want to take you to see my mom in Savannah. How long can you stay?"

"As long as I want," Constance says.

"Ok."

"I'm not going back to Grandma's."

"Why not?"

"I don't want to live with her; I was just glad to finally meet her."

"Okay," AJ says. "Have you told her?"

"I'll call her tonight."

"You can call now." AJ reaches over and picks up the cordless phone off the table between the two rockers and hands it to Constance. "I'm sure she's worried about you."

Constance smiles, takes AJ's phone, dials a bogus number, waits a moment, and then says, "No answer." She hangs up and says, "Thanks, cuz. I'll try again later. Will you help me find a place to stay in my price range? I can't afford much."

"Don't be silly," AJ says. "You can stay here. Actually, it would be nice to have family here without having to drive to Savannah; everyone else is even farther away."

"Sounds like living here is lonely," Constance says.

"Well, my husband is on the other side of the world, and I'm raising three kids alone; the closest family to me is Mom in Savannah, so I guess it is a little lonely."

Constance turns her face away from AJ and smiles. She thinks, *Once again I'm safe. She has not talked to Mae.* Then she looks around the room at the furniture and more family pictures on the wall and says, "Give me your life. I'll take it."

AJ laughs and says, "Trust me; with a seventeen-, fifteen-, and thirteen-year-old, there's more to it than it seems. But I do thank God for it every day."

"You don't look like you've had one kid, and you've have three?" says Constance.

"Well, thank you," AJ replies. "Thomas is seventeen; Monica is fifteen, and Ike is thirteen. They're hanging out with friends now but they'll be home soon. Now, we will visit Mom tomorrow. She'll be so happy to see you. Then we will start looking for the perfect job for you."

Constance turns her head and tightens her lips in a victory celebration, as that is just what she wanted to hear.

"I'm not expecting to live here for free. I'll pay you something. Sorry, I'm no good at cooking, but I can clean."

"Listen," AJ says, "the kids all have their chores. Just clean behind yourself, and that will be fine." She shakes her head. "And no, you will not pay me. I believe in helping people help themselves. You will be able to move out on your own sooner if you are able to save your money. Besides, all the kids have jobs and are working towards the same goal: moving out one day."

*   *   *

Two weeks go by, and while Constance is getting on with her life in Atlanta, Steven arrives at the duplex each morning and checks his mail and his voice messages, hoping for some communication from Constance. When he realizes there is no message, he sits quietly with his teeth clenched, shaking his head, before he starts his day. Monday morning of the third week, he gathers a stack of mail from the duplex lockbox. He walks down the hallway to his office and sits at his desk. He looks through the stack of mail in his hand, dropping the tenant payments onto his desk.

Then he notices that one of the envelopes is from a credit card company. He stares at the envelope, thinking someone's mail was delivered to him in error, but he sees that it is addressed to him. He notices another letter addressed to him, from another credit card company. He looks at the last piece of mail, which is a utility bill. He drops the utility bill on the desk.

Steven opens the first credit card statement. He sees his name on the account, which has a $1,500 credit limit; the card is maxed out and the first payment is overdue. He opens the second statement, which shows a $1,000 credit limit; this card is maxed out as well, and the first payment is overdue. He stares at both letters, thinking ...

Instantly he knows it was Constance. She is the only person who has had that type of access to him. Holding the bills in his hands, he says, "Well, I'll be ..."

He slams the letters down on his desk and shakes his head, thinking about how he had started to check her application but never finished. He had no reason to suspect her; she was a model employee and a Christian woman—as far as he knew.

He reaches into his drawer and finds her application. He scans it for a telephone number and dials the number. A man answers.

"Hello?"

"Is Constance there?" Steven asks.

"You got the wrong number," the man says, hanging up the phone.

Steven curses as he throws the application in the trash. He thinks about how stupid he has been; he thought it was strange that she never talked about herself or family except to say they were very private. At the time, he didn't think much about that, because he could relate; he considered himself very private too.

He recalls how she never wanted a ride home. He looks at the application in the trash and says, "I bet the address is phony, too." Then he curses again, gets up from his desk, locks the office, and leaves.

*   *   *

Constance is the perfect houseguest her first week with AJ. Her cousin takes off from work the first three days so they can get acquainted. On Monday of the second week, AJ returns to working her long hours and traveling. Constance converts back to her real self—the one she told herself was forgotten because she was going to be a normal person when she reached AJ's home.

On Monday after AJ leaves for work, Constance puts on a two-piece suit and stands at Thomas's bedroom door, watching him type on his laptop. "Will you please do me a favor?" she asks. When he looks up, she says, "Can you take me job hunting?"

"Sure," he says and quickly grabs his keys. They leave the house around nine o'clock. Constance looks for jobs all over Atlanta until noon. She tells Thomas she is starving, so he takes her to a restaurant for lunch. After lunch, she resumes job searching. By three o'clock, they return home. Tuesday she asks him to take her job hunting again. When they get in his car, she tells him where she needs to go, but these are home addresses, not businesses. Reluctantly, he takes her everywhere she asks.

Wednesday morning, Constance is dressed and standing in Thomas's bedroom doorway with a briefcase in her hand. Thomas is lying on his bed, working on his laptop. He looks up and sees her standing there.

"I don't have any money," Thomas says, "and my car doesn't drive off air."

Looking sorrowful and desperate, Constance says, "I just know I'm going to get a job today. I prayed, and I'm trusting in faith. It's mine. Please, Thomas, I don't have any other way."

"It better work out for you," Thomas says harshly. "This is the last time."

He closes his laptop, gets off the bed, and walks quickly out the door; she steps aside to keep from bumping into him.

Monica comes out of her room when she hears her brother and Constance walk down the hall. She calls Constance over; Constance, irritated by the interruption, stops at the front door.

"Have you seen my earrings?" Monica asks. "They were on my dresser, and now I can't find them."

Holding the doorknob, Constance says sharply, "No. Maybe your mom has them."

Monica places her right hand on her hip and stares at Constance.

"My mother's ears are not pierced," she snaps back.

As Constance closes the door, she calls back, "Sorry, don't have them. Gotta go."

On the way to the job interview, Constance talks Thomas into stopping at a house in an area of town he never goes to.

"Who do you know over here?" Thomas asks. "I wouldn't be caught dead in this neighborhood."

Constance ignores him. "Turn here and pull up to the yellow house," she says.

Thomas turns the car sharply and stops in front of the yellow house.

"You just got here. How'd you find out about this place?"

"You ask too many questions," Constance says. "I'll be back in a minute so we can go."

She slams the car door.

Thomas yells through the glass as she walks away, "Where? To a job interview?" Thomas says to himself, "Liar. Faith, huh. She loves Jesus, all right. I should leave her here."

After what seems like forever, Thomas looks up from his hunched over position at the steering wheel and sees her fluffing her hair, and then she opens her purse, places her hand in her pocket, pulls out a wad of cash and drops it in her purse, all the while she is walking back to the car very quickly. She gets in and slams the door. Thomas starts the car and angrily drives off.

"Where's this interview?" he says. "I have other things to do on my day off than drive you all over town."

"Forget it," Constance says in a nasty tone. "That took so long, I know it is too late."

Furious, Thomas yells, "I knew it. You were lying! That's it!"

"You'll take me wherever I need to go," Constance yells back. "And don't think about tellin' your mama, or I'll just have to tell her about your drug dealin.'"

"What? You crazy?" he says. "My mother knows me better than that."

"You underestimate me," Constance says very calmly, keeping her eyes on the road. "I've already planted drugs in your room and this car. You won't find them, but I'll make sure ya mama will. Now do what you're told and drive me home. I'm tired."

Thomas is steaming mad, but he holds his peace. He drives home, rushes out of the car to his room, and slams the door.

His mother had told her children that Constance was going to be staying with them for a while, and to make her feel welcome. But all that ended that day.

When he calms down, he asks Monica and Ike to come to his room so they can talk. They each begin to talk about Constance and what they think of her. They are sure it is Constance who is stealing from them, not each other. They discuss everything and wait anxiously for their mother to get home from work so they can tell her.

While they are in Thomas's room, they hear shouting outside on the porch. They walk into the foyer and see Constance standing at the front door, arguing with a lady outside.

The three of them walk toward Constance, and the lady looks around Constance and sees them. She looks at all three of them as they look at her.

She turns her focus to Constance and says, "I'll be back."

She walks away.

Constance slams the door, walks past the kids to her room, and starts packing her things. When she's done, she calls a cab and leaves too. She says nothing about where she is going.

As quickly as she came to AJ's, she is gone.

AJ arrives home from work, looking for a big hello from her kids like she usually gets.

"Hey, where is everyone?" she yells out.

Thomas, Monica, and Ike come from the back of the house and pour their hearts out to their mom.

"Mama," Thomas says. "Constance is not who you think she is. She is Satan reincarnated."

AJ quickly moves into her disciplinary character and says, "Boy, that's not how I've raised you to talk. Now what's going on?"

"Yeah, Mama," Monica chimes in. "She's a big liar. Every time I asked her if she had something of mine, she would say, 'Maybe your mama has it.' I know she took my clothes and jewelry."

AJ is now perplexed. Her kids are acting totally out of character. She is moved to silence.

Ike says, "I saw her stealing my money, and she threatened me, saying she would tell you I was selling drugs if I said anything."

AJ tries to speak, but she can't get one word out.

Monica chimes in again and says, "I came home from school, and she was letting some man out the back door. When I asked what he was doing in our house, she said he was not in the house. She said she gave him some food because he was homeless. He didn't seem homeless to me. He went down the street and got in a Grand Am and drove away."

"She lied about everything," Thomas says, "and she used that drug line on me too. Mama, she never went to any interviews. She had me to drive her to people's houses and wait in the car in parts of town I would not be caught dead in."

Ike chimes in again, "All I did every day was clean behind her. I knew she was going to blame her mess on me. I hope she don't come back."

AJ is too devastated to speak. All she can do is drop her head in disgust.

Talking out loud to herself, she says, "I let her into my home and treated her like family, and she treated me like dirt. Where is she now?"

Thomas, Monica, and Ike said in chorus, "A lady came to the door about an hour ago—"

AJ interrupts them, "A lady? What lady, Thomas?"

"All we know," Thomas says, "is that Constance was shouting at this lady on the porch. By the time we got to the front door, the lady looked mad and said she would be back and left. Constance quickly packed her stuff—"

"And some of mine," Monica interrupts quickly.

"And she left," Thomas finishes his sentence. "Ma, she's not coming back. That lady was mad, and Constance knew it."

"My God, my God," AJ says. "Forgive me, Father God, for the thoughts I have." She looks at each child and says, "Why didn't you tell me? I would never allow anything like this in my home. I am so mad right now, I would hurt her. I thank God she is not here."

Before AJ could finish talking, the doorbell rings. She jumps up and answers the door.

A slim woman with short brown curly hair and a serious look on her face says, "Hello, is Constance here?"

Checking the lady out, AJ says slowly, "Who are you?"

"My name is Julie. Listen, I am a Christian woman. I don't mean any harm by coming to your home. I know you don't know me." All three kids follow AJ and stand behind her.

"Mama," Monica says. "This is the lady who was here earlier."

"Yes, I was," Julie says quickly. "I was talking to Constance, but when I realized there were children here, I decided to leave. Is she here?"

"No," AJ says.

"May I please speak with you?" Julie asks.

AJ looks at Julie and says, "Come on in."

Julie steps inside the door, glances over at the kids, and then says, "Constance says this is her home."

"No," AJ says, "she is my cousin. I was putting her up for a while."

Julie looks at the kids again and then whispers to AJ, "Your cousin is having an affair with my brother, who is married. I don't blame her; I blame him. But he brought her into my home, and she stole money from my bedridden mother. I know it was her." She pulls a videotape out of her purse. "I'm sure my crazy brother brought her over to show her off to my mother.

"I'm my mother's caregiver. She has Alzheimer's. I work long hours, so I hire aides to come in and sit with her. I installed a video camera in her room to keep watch on her and see how the aides treat her. No one knows it's there but me. My brother left Constance in her room, and this tape shows her going through her things." Julie is still holding up the videotape. "I'm letting you know, because I'm on my way to file a police report."

"I am so sorry," AJ says.

"You seem like a nice person," Julie says. "You shouldn't have her living around your kids. She's a liar. My brother says she's a sweet Christian girl. Huh, she's not who she pretends to be."

AJ looks back at Thomas and then turns back to Julie, saying, "Trust me, she no longer lives here."

Julie places the tape back in her purse.

"Well, I just wanted to let you know. I don't appreciate being violated. I'm not going to take it. Let her know."

Julie leaves.

While making dinner, AJ asks the children to tell her everything. Thomas, Monica, and Ike each sit at the counter while their mother stands at the range, stirring a big pot of spaghetti. AJ looks at Ike first.

Ike quickly says, "Mama, I don't like her. She, she always was mean to me."

"Slow down, son," AJ replies, as she adds extra sauce to the pot.

Ike starts again, quickly trying to get his words out. AJ holds up one hand, while holding on to the glass bottle of sauce with the other hand, and slowly says, "Stop. Breathe," placing the sauce container on the counter.

Ike takes a deep breath and starts again slowly, "She asks me every day to throw something in the garbage for her, take something to the laundry room, bring her something out of the refrigerator, or pick up something."

"Like what?" AJ asks.

"Her shoes, her purse, a magazine. She just use me."

AJ bites her lip and says, "I'm sorry, baby," and then she holds out her arms for Ike to come and give her a huge.

While she leans down and gives Ike a big hug, she looks over at Monica.

"I know you said we should not hate anyone, but I hate her," Monica says.

AJ releases Ike and looks Monica directly in her eyes.

"I do, Mama. You said we're not supposed to steal, but she does. I'm missing some of my favorite shirts and jewelry. Where is it, if she doesn't have it? She was always telling me"—Monica attempts to speak like Constance—"'Maybe your mom has it.' She's a liar and thief."

"Honey, sort through your clothes and jewelry, and tell me everything that's missing," AJ says to Monica with an I-love-you smile on her face.

"Okay," Monica says as she smiles back.

AJ gives Monica a hug and kiss and tells her and Ike to go wash up for dinner. As soon as they leave, she says to Thomas, "Do I need to sit down?"

"Yes, ma' am," he replies, as AJ sits on the stool next to him.

"Don't leave anything out, son," she says before Thomas starts speaking.

"She would say she had a job interview, but after we got in the car, all of a sudden she just had to stop somewhere first. She knew every back alley and rough-neck place in town. Places I wouldn't be caught dead in. But I'm there waiting for her to come out so she can go to her job interview. She never went to one job interview. She just begged all of us for money."

"All of you were giving her money?" AJ asks in disgust.

"I didn't know Ike and Monica was until today. I thought it was just me," he replies.

"Why were you?" AJ asks.

"Because I thought you wanted us to help her. Mama, you said she had had hard times and needed her family, and you wanted us to try real hard and help her."

"I was talking about her staying with us. I know you all are not used to having a stranger in the house. I wanted you all to think of her as family and not a stranger. How much did you give her? No. Don't tell me. Get ready for dinner; we'll talk about this later."

Monica and Ike return to the kitchen just as Thomas walks out to go and wash his hands. AJ gets off the bar stool and walks over to the refrigerator and pulls out a big bowl of salad and three bottles of dressing and places all of it on the counter.

"Fix your brother's plate," she says to Monica as she walks out of the kitchen. She walks to her room, closes the door, and begins to cry. She paces for a moment and then sits on her bed; she picks up the phone on her night stand and calls her mother. The answering machine comes on; AJ, crying as she speaks, says, "Mom, if you're there, pick up."

Vivian picks up the phone and says, "Honey? I was in another room. What's going on?"

"Ma, I'm so mad, I could hurt her."

"Constance?" her mom says with certainty.

"Yes. I treated her like family and she has treated me like dirt."

"This is my fault. I should have told you not to let her stay with you."

"No, Ma. I know about her life. I thought she really wanted help. She had Thomas driving her all over Atlanta, taking her to stranger's houses and back alleys."

"For what?"

"I don't Ma; maybe drugs; I don't know."

"Why did he take her?"

"Oh, he didn't just take her; he waited on her and gave her money."

"It's my sister's fault this child is like she is."

"I know, Ma, but I don't feel sorry for her right now. I was trying to help her. Right now I could kill her; she even took money from my baby. Ike said, 'Mama, she just use me.'" The tears roll down AJ's cheek and she quickly wipes them.

"I'm coming over this weekend and get my grandchildren and talk to them," Vivian says. "Baby, I'm sorry. Where is she now?"

"Far away from here," AJ replies.

"Are you sure?"

"I'm sure. She stole from some lady and the lady came here."

"What? I'm sorry to say this, but call the police."

"The lady already did. I got a headache. I'm going to lay down and try and sleep this off. I'll call you tomorrow."

"If she comes back there, you call the police."

"I will; love you. Good night," AJ says before hanging up. She slowly places the phone on the receiver and lays across her bed.

Chapter 5
A Last Resort

When Constance left AJ's home, she went to the airport and purchased a one-way ticket to Jacksonville, Florida. She remembered reading an article about Jacksonville and its beaches in the Successful Woman magazine she purchased in Charleston.

This is a good idea, she thinks, since I have no family in Florida. I desperately need to get away from this lifestyle. I know my family hates me. I didn't mean to con them. Why can't I let this go? I want to be different. It was truly never her intention to treat any of her family members the way she has. She realizes the lifestyle she lives is rooted in her mother's character.

She thinks about how she left her mother and brother in the heat of anger and how she cunningly picked the relatives she wanted to stay with. She knew Mae has wanted her to come for a visit since she was a child. She believed her father's mother wanted to get to know her and spend time with her. And she chose AJ because she knew Aunt Vivian has always wanted the two of them to be close.

Her very inner essence seems to be working out her schemes and cons with little or no effort when all she wants is to be a different person than she is and to live a better lifestyle, an honest, decent life. She honestly thought she could live with her relatives and leave her old ways behind. It was only after she lived with Mae for a few weeks that she found herself fighting the con within and ultimately giving into it, as she found it so easy to do. And the same thing happened when she was with Grandma Wilts and again with AJ. She realizes she is too rooted in the con life she thought she could easily leave behind.

Now, all she can think about is that she is doomed with both sides of her family. Although Mae and AJ only talk at family reunions every two years, Constance is sure all of the family will be talking now. She basically has no friends, and she figures that, between Mae, Steven, and AJ, she'd better disappear.

As Constance boards the plane, she notices the muscular young man in front of her; his physique and cologne are so intriguing, she wants to hug him and not let go. Even the stewardess seems to share her sentiments: She looks at the man's ticket, says, "Welcome aboard, Mr. Greene," and escorts him to first class. Constance takes her seat in the coach area, thinking about how much she hated her life with her mother and wanted to be free from it, yet she is still living the life her mother exposed her to by conning and running.

When Constance gets to Jacksonville, she makes sure to use her money sparingly and finds the local women's shelter and stays there. After a couple of nights in the shelter, she decides that she is not going to live another day in that place. When the manager of the shelter arrives the next morning with the newspaper, Constance asks for the classifieds. She sits and looks through the housing advertisements.

She reads and marks and reads and marks. Everything she wants is out of her reach thus far, but she knows she can finagle her way into something, if necessary. Finally, she sees something that lights a smile in her. This smile starts in her inner being and reflects on her face. She has found the perfect advertisement. It has her name all over it.

In very small, bold print on the last page of the classifieds, located at the bottom of the page was written:

ROOMMATE WANTED. SINGLE GUY SEEKING FEMALE ROOMMATE TO SHARE A TWO-BEDROOM, TWO-BATH, FULLY FURNISHED TOWNHOME. RENT, UTILITIES AND WATER—ALL INCLUDED FOR ONLY $175 MONTHLY. CALL 555-1234.

Constance drops the pen, tears out that portion of the paper, and hurries to ask to use the shelter's phone. She makes the call and finds out that the place is still available.

That day, she moves in with the single guy. All she can think about is that no one knows where she is, and she is glad. The guy lives in an upscale neighborhood. The living room separates each bedroom and bathroom. The place is immaculate. The guy is handsome, muscular, and very distinguished with a deep voice. He tells her to call him Tony.

Constance places her luggage bag in the extra bedroom and quickly makes her way back to the living room to talk with Tony.

She notices how well coordinated the place is. There is a black leather sofa, loveseat, and recliner furniture set, which is well coordinated with a black, brown, and gold area rug on top of shiny, hardwood floors. The beige walls add charm to the matching lamps on their fancy lamp stands around the furniture.

There is a bookcase full of books. There is a flat screen television mounted on the wall opposite from the bookcase, and there are two tall, standing lamps—one on each side of the flat screen television. A small magazine rack separates the recliner from the leather sofa, and it is filled with magazines. The room has no pictures, paintings, flowers, or anything to necessarily suggest a woman's touch, yet it is so well coordinated it makes her think there must be someone.

Constance is flabbergasted by the fact that, just an hour or so ago, she was one of the twenty residents of a women's shelter with a concrete floor, folding chairs, mats overlaying wooden frames for bedding, dim lighting, and one small, black-and-white television located in a corner. Now, she is a handsome young man's roommate in a prestigious townhome in an upscale area of the city.

Constance sits down on the leather sofa.

"I feel like God has blessed me with you," she says to Tony. "You're the only person I have in the world."

Tony is sitting back in the recliner. He looks at her in disbelief and, with a half laugh, says, "Don't you think you're exaggerating your situation a bit?"

Constance goes right into the man-charming, sophisticated character that has worked to her benefit all of her life; sounding innocent, she says, "No, I'm not. My family is not there for me. But God is, and he alone is my one need."

Tony sits up in the recliner and looks at Constance. With a calm, serious voice, he says, "Don't try to convince me you love the Lord. If you do, it will show. I love him too, but you don't hear me trying to convince you." He drops his head for a moment. Then he looks again at Constance and says, "Here's the deal: You can stay here, but you must pay your way."

Constance leans forward on the sofa and, with a half-smile, says, "I always pay my way. No problem."

Tony looks at her for a moment. He puts his hands together and brings them up to his mouth. Then he says, "Let me make myself plain and clear. You will not pay your way by offering me your body. You pay your way with a job. Keep your body to yourself."

Constance sighs, mixed with a laugh, as she frowns and says, "I'm just grateful to God for you helping me out in my time of need. I only meant I always pay my way, that's all. I'm not thinking about offering you my body."

Tony says sarcastically, "Of course you're not," and leaves the room.

The same week she moves in with Tony, Constance gets a job at the neighborhood grocery store, working the night shift. Three months go by quickly, and all that time, she watches Tony come and go with no one around.

She thinks to herself, Tony and I have been roommates for three months, and he has not even really looked at me. I just see him in passing. He seems to be nice. I know he's straightforward and a real man. How is he able to live with me like this? He acts like he isn't even attracted to me. He seems so in control and definitely maintains his composure. He's a man that handles his business. I really like that. But I've never had a man around me that was not trying to get with me.

This was new to Constance. She never sees him with a woman. No one calls him at the house. The only mail that comes are bills, so she starts to think about how she can get him to take an interest in her. She knows he is smart. She likes that he is well-educated, and she can tell he cannot be conned easily. She decides to show him how wonderful she is, that she is perfect for him. She is glad that she decided to move to Jacksonville. She is glad no one else in this city knows her.

Although she has no friends here, she decides to be cautious and not assume someone doesn't know her. She feels it is best to keep to herself. She has always heard her mother say how small the world really is; she does not let anyone get close to her, because they just might know her past. She realizes this is one time she agrees with her mother, and she certainly does not want anyone to be able to link her back to her family and the life she left behind.

However, she does bond with one coworker, Spree, another cashier. They work the same shift, and Spree prides herself on being Miss Congeniality and Miss Know-It-All—all rolled into one package.

One night, there is not a soul in the store. This is rare, as the store is usually packed with shoppers until it closes at midnight, and even then, last-minute customers beat on the door, talking through the glass, trying to explain their desperate situations in the hope of getting in. But this night, around nine o'clock, there is not a customer to be found. Constance's mind, as usual, is on Tony. She walks over to Spree's register, and they converse.

"Can you believe the store is empty?" Constance asks.

"I know, right? Makes you wonder what's goin' on," Spree says.

"We deserve this break."

"True that. I'll call and give some man advice."

"What? You're the expert?"

"The one and only. Girl, I should have written my book by now: Man: The Final Frontier: How to Go Where No Woman Has Gone Before."

Constance laughs.

"You see this phone?" Spree says. "It's full of numbers. I've helped some get married, saved some marriages. And some I've helped to leave. There was no need for them to even think about stayin'." Spree hands Constance her cell phone and says, "Pick a number, any number."

Constance smiles, takes the phone, and says, "This is a nice cell phone."

"Let me show you something," Spree says. She clicks on her address book and hands the phone back to Constance.

"How many numbers do you have in here?" Constance asks as she scrolls through all the names.

"You wasting time," Spree says. "Call one, and ask if I helped them."

A woman walks in the door, gets a shopping cart, and heads toward the back of the store. Constance and Spree look up at her. Constance hands Spree back her phone.

"She gonna be a while. Did you see that box of coupons she had?"

"Yeah," Spree says.

Still standing at Spree's register, Constance says, "Okay, Miss Expert, how can you tell if a man has a special woman in his life?"

Spree moves right into her Miss Know-It-All attitude and says, "The signs!"

Constance just stares at her.

Spree looks at the blank expression on Constance's face and says, "Let me help you. You will see one of these seven signs if there is a special woman in a man's life:

"One: He will smell of her perfume.

"Two: His voice will change when he's talking to her on the phone.

"Three: Her voice will be on his answering machine.

"Four: Her number will be on caller ID at least twenty times.

"Five: His cell phone bill will be loaded with her number, especially late at night.

"Six: There will be something of hers at his place—perfume, clothing, undergarments, lingerie, hair products, the unmentionables ... girl, even a barrette.

"Seven: He will have a card, love letter, or gift wrappings, and definitely some red wine, martini, or margaritas in his fridge—you know, drinks a woman likes, sweet and fruity. Men drink the hard stuff.

"Oh and by the way, number eight," she says while rolling her eyes confidently, "if you can get your hands on one of his bank statements or credit card bills, he has wined and dined her or bought something for her, especially during the holidays. All you need is to check out the signs," Spree repeats as she snaps her fingers.

The customer finally makes her way to the front. Constance walks back to her register. While Spree rings the customer up, she looks over at Constance, raises her eyebrows, and nods at Constance as though to say, "I know I'm right."

The first opportunity Constance gets, she takes advantage of Spree's advice and checks for the signs. There are absolutely no signs—not even one. In her last place to search, she goes to a small table in Tony's bedroom. She finds a credit card bill and bank statement. After reviewing them and not seeing any purchases that would suggest female gifts or clothing, she thinks to herself, How can he just have one bank statement and one credit card bill? And these are from last year. Where are the others? She carefully places them back in his drawer and closes it.

The day after her search, Constance talks with Spree again.

"So you say the signs will never fail?" Constance asks.

"Never," Spree says.

"And if there are no signs?"

"If he is a real man, he's obviously been hurt; he's taking time to get himself together. It won't be long. Someone will cross his path, and he will recover, but for now, he's single."

Two weeks later, Constance comes in from working her night shift, and for once, Tony is there. Anxious to know if she can break his icy position with her, she comes right in and starts her questioning.

"Well, hello, stranger. I know it's none of my business, but I was wondering, where do you attend church? Maybe we can go together."

Tony is sitting in the recliner, watching a basketball game on television. He never looks at her as he answers calmly, "No, we can't. I told you when you first moved in, I'm giving you a place to stay, and that's it."

Constance sits on the sofa and removes her purse from her shoulder.

"I know. It's just that I never see you with anyone, and I was thinking since I don't have anyone, maybe we can do some things together, you know, as friends."

Still watching television, Tony says, "You don't have any friends?"

Constance sits back on the sofa and sighs. "Not really," she says. "All my friends are back home. You know I work at night. That doesn't leave me a lot of time to meet people." She looks down and says, "And I'm lonely." Then she looks up and finds Tony looking at her.

With a blank face and calm voice, Tony says, "Well, I'm not. I like my life just as it is—private."

Constance thinks to herself, This doesn't happen to me. She looks at him seriously and asks, "So you do have someone?"

With the same calm tone, Tony says, "Did I say that?"

Constance shakes her head.

"No, but—" she starts to speak, but Tony cuts her off.

"Constance, if it's getting to be too much for you to live here, maybe you need to find yourself another place."

Constance's stomach drops. She puts up a brave front with a half-smile and says, "No!" She raises her hands and says, "I'm okay. Look, I promise I'll stay out of your business. Sorry I asked. It won't happen again. I don't have enough money to move, but I am working on it."

"Okay," Tony says.

He gets up and leaves the room.

Constance is flabbergasted. She can't believe what just happened to her. Since her mother started forcing her at age twelve to have sex with men, she has never had a man resist her or not desire her. Men always stare at her and grope at her shapely figure. She is amazed that Tony doesn't even care to look at her. She thinks to herself, Who is this man? Now more than ever, she wants him. She feels frustrated and challenged by the unusual and unfamiliar lack of reaction on Tony's part. She sits, thinking, and decides she is not remotely considering moving out. Her thoughts are only about what she needs to do to get his attention.

When she hears the front door close, she knows Tony has left, but that doesn't matter to her. She reminds herself that she is his roommate. No one else lives with them, and there are no signs of another woman. She allows her thoughts to drift to the life she really wants: she desires to be his wife. She wishes she did not have the past she has and hopes he never finds out.

Her heart is lusting. Her body is burning with desire for him, but she has no idea how she can get him to even look at her, not to mention take an interest in her. She thinks to herself, I feel like I'm in a living hell. How can he be so close and so far away at the same time? I thought men were pawns to be played and used—never taken seriously. But this man is like no other. How can he be so different? Who is he really? She decides she has to have him, and she is going to have him. She thinks to herself, I didn't end up as his roommate by chance. This is my blessing. I'm going to pray that God will give me the desire of my heart.

She gets up from the sofa, goes to her bedroom, and kneels down beside her bed. She places her hands together in preparation for prayer and takes a deep breath. As soon as she closes her eyes, she instantly thinks about every person she has recently used—Mae, Grandma, Steven, AJ, Thomas, Monica, Ike, and Julie's brother and mother. Her actions, along with their faces, flash in her mind like she is watching a movie. She stays in her kneeling position, waiting to start her prayer. The longer she kneels, the more she feels undeserving of the prayer she wants to pray. Unworthiness finally overwhelms her.

"God," she says. "I don't know you. I'll just change myself." She gets up off her knees.

She knows Tony is well educated and figures he must love to read books, because he has so many. She goes about changing everything about herself.

Physically, she changes her hairstyle, joins a health club, and hires the club's top personal trainer. She buys new clothes—only designer, as she notices Tony is a man of good taste.

She exhausts the money she stole from Mae, Steven, AJ's kids, and Julie's mother. She even uses up the money she earned from working with Steven, which she had not had to use, because Grandma Wilts would not allow her to pay for anything. All in all, it is a decent amount of money—enough to help anyone get on their feet. But her change is costly, and although she had done so well in not using it before, when she decides to change herself, it goes like water. She isn't making much at her current job, but she uses that too.

She starts going to church every Sunday morning. She even goes to some night services on the Sundays she is lucky enough to have the day off. She reads all types of books and magazines—the Bible, motivational, business, spiritual growth, child-rearing, health, bodybuilding and sculpting, history, Sports Illustrated, camping, gardening, and fishing. You name it, she buys it and reads it.

She purposely lets Tony see her watching sports events on television and reading her Bible. She always makes sure to leave her bedroom door open on the nights he is home watching television in the living room, so he can hear her praying. She is happy for the times she leaves for church service and she can speak to him in passing.

With all that she does, Tony remains the same, and she falls into a deep despair that she will never win him over.

Chapter 6
The Blind Side

One Friday night, Constance is scheduled to work the late shift as one of the closing cashiers. Her boss tells her she can leave early, because they are slow. She clocks out and leaves. When she gets home, Tony is not there, as usual.

Instead of staying home to eat, she decides to go out to a local restaurant. She goes to her room and starts looking through her closet, trying to decide what to wear. As she picks out a dress, she thinks about where she will go. She has heard about this one place and how nice it is ... although it's a little pricey. But she feels she deserves it, since she recently got a raise. She pulls a sexy, black dress that is well fitted over her head. It hangs three inches above her knees. She fix her hair and puts on makeup.

"I'm Tony's girl," she says to the mirror. "No need to drive men too crazy." She slips on her black pumps and calls a cab.

She gets in the cab and tells the driver, "Finer Dining Restaurant downtown, please." When the cab pulls up to the restaurant, she notices the classy Art Nouveau architecture incasing the beautiful glass doors. She pays the cab driver and reaches for her door handle to open it. Before she can open it, the door is opened and a man dressed in a black jacket, white shirt, and black bow tie leans down, smiles, and says, "Welcome to Finer Dining restaurant." He reaches for her hand and gently pulls her out of the cab and closes the door. He extends his elbow to her and escorts her to the front door. "My lady is most beautiful tonight," he says as they reach the doors, which open automatically. He extends her hand to another gentlemen dressed the same way. "You have a choice of seating tonight, madam," the second man says, leading her into the dining area.

Constance smiles at him and looks around the restaurant. It has beautiful oak tables and chairs. There are candles on each table that give the place an ambiance and coziness. There are only a few patrons in the restaurant. Constance points to a table in the corner. The man walks her over to the table, says, "Your waiter will be with you in just a moment; enjoy your meal," and then walks away.

Less than a minute later, her waiter walks up, hands her a menu, and says, "Madam, welcome. My name is Kai; may I get you a drink?"

"A glass of red wine, please," she says, taking the menu.

"Certainly," he says and walks away.

Constance holds the menu and looks around the place. She smiles as she thinks, This is just what I needed—to be pampered.

Kai returns in a minute with a chilled glass of red wine. "Are you ready to order?" he asks.

Not wanting to seem a novice to this type of dining, she quickly opens the menu and replies, "Lobster Fra Diablo."

Kai nods and walks away. She sits quietly, enjoying the décor, and sips her wine. She glimpses at her watch; it's eight thirty. Her meal arrives, and she starts to eat, thinking her usual thoughts: I'm going to make this man my husband. She takes her time, making sure to eat slowly.

By nine o'clock, the restaurant has filled up, and a young lady—beautiful, very curvaceous, and well dressed—is standing with the waiter, looking in her direction.

The waiter walks over to Constance's table and says, "Madam, please forgive me, the madam over there," he points at the lady, "asks, if you are not waiting for anyone, can she please share this table with you?"

Constance gently nods at the lady and says to the waiter, "Sure. No problem."

The young lady walks over and sits down. "Thank you," she says. "I love this place and usually don't have a problem getting a table. I'm Frances."

"Hello, my name is Constance."

"Do you eat here often?"

"No," Constance says. "I rarely eat out. I just didn't feel like cooking tonight."

Frances laughs and says, "Believe me, I understand. Truth be told, I never cook. I live with my cousin; she does all the cooking."

"That's best, you know," Constance says. "Home-cooked meals are more nutritional."

Frances nods and says, "I agree. I have been so spoiled by my cousin's love of cooking. I need to start cooking for myself."

"It's easy," Constance says. "If you read up on the benefits of preparing healthy meals at home, I'm sure you'll develop a love for it."

"Is that how you came to love it?"

"Yes," Constance replies, still nibbling at her meal.

Frances sits quietly for a moment and then says, "My good thing has come to an end. So I guess I'll have to start cooking too."

Constance asks, "Why?"

"My cousin is moving out tomorrow," says Frances, "and I know I'm either going to have to start cooking or find another roommate who cooks."

The waiter returns with Frances's water, and she places her order.

As the waiter walks away, Frances looks serious, but she says, in a joking way, "Are you looking for a roommate?"

Constance shakes her head and says, "No." After another sip of her drink, she says, "I have one for now." Smiling, she continues, "But I know it is going to be so much more. My roommate is a wonderful man."

Frances widens her eyes and then says, "I tell you, I don't know what's in the air, but my cousin caught it too. She is in love with a wonderful man. He loves her so much; he has gone all out to show her he is able to control himself in any situation."

Taking a bite of food, Constance says, "Really?"

"Yes," Frances says. "My cousin is a good person, and he knows that. She told him she has no desire to be in a relationship with just any man. She wants a man who has the qualities she is looking for. As silly as it seems, she told him that all her other serious relationships ended because her mates couldn't be trusted around other women."

"I would have never told him that," Constance says. "He may have felt like there is something wrong with her."

"Exactly," Frances says. "Anyway, she told him, and they made this pact that, if he could control himself around other women, she would know he was the man for her. Is that not the craziest thing you've ever heard of?"

"Yes," Constance says, still eating. "How would she know if he was truthful or not? What would he have to do?"

"He got himself a roommate," Frances says, lowering her voice. "I tell you, he loves my cousin to death. I don't understand it. It's crazy and senseless, but she said she would only have a man in her life that she could trust. He decided she was worth him proving himself, so they agreed."

Constance stops eating and looks at Frances with a frown and says, "To what? A roommate?"

Frances leans closer to Constance, lowers her voice even more, and then says, "Yes. You're not going to believe me, but I'm going to tell you anyway. His roommate works the night shift at some grocery store. When the roommate is not there, he and my cousin spend a few hours at his place. But most of his time is spent at our place.

"This craziness has been going on for six months. My cousin finally said yes to his marriage proposal last month. He didn't know, but she was planning the wedding all the while he was proving himself. So, as they say, Wa-la. Tomorrow they will be Mr. and Mrs." Frances stated his name—his full, total name: "Reginald Antonio Anderson."

Constance has seen Tony's name on a couple of pieces of his mail as she was snooping around his personal belongings, looking for signs of a woman. All Constance can think is, It's Tony. It's Tony. It's Tony! She is sick. She cannot speak. She cannot move. She cannot breathe. She wants to get out of there, scream, die. But her body does nothing but sink into the depths of her internal hell.

Did you come here to seal my doom? Constance thinks, looking at Frances. Do you know you just cut open my chest and cut out my heart?

Frances keeps talking, but Constance honestly cannot hear a word she says.

Then in a sick, seemingly planned, and very well-orchestrated way, Frances looks at her watch and says, "Oh my goodness, look at the time. I've got to go. I'm the maid of honor, and I must get to the hotel to get my beauty rest."

At that same moment, the waiter returns with Frances' meal, and she says to him, "I'm going to take this to go."

The waiter walks away with the meal to package it in a to-go box.

Frances stands up, picks up her purse, and says to Constance, "It was nice meeting you. Thanks for letting me sit with you and burn up your ear. And good luck on that wonderful roommate of yours becoming your man."

She smiles and is gone as quickly as she came.

Constance is sick. These are the thoughts that consume her mind, one right after the other, giving her no relief: Did she know I'm his roommate? Did she care? She never asked me anything about my roommate. Does she know me? Is this a sick joke? Did Tony send her here? Did he know all along I was falling for him? I can't believe this is happening. I need help. Someone! Anyone! Please help me! Oh my God!

Karma had finally reached her, and landed directly on her heart. Constance's internal cry starts out strong within her, but her pain is so overwhelming she cannot even maintain an internal scream. With almost no mental or physical strength, she manages to gather herself and stands, lays some money on the table next to her plate, and leaves the restaurant. She rushes to the side of the building and throws up.

Somehow she manages to calm herself and begins walking home. It is dark and late, yet that is no concern to her. Tony's apartment is seventeen blocks away; even that did not cross her mind. She stumbles home as though she is a zombie in a drunken stupor. She almost gets hit by a car, and it does not matter to her. Constance is in agony.

Worse yet, when she finally wanders home that night, the walls of the apartment seem to close in on her. For the rest of that night, through Saturday and Sunday, Tony does not come back to the apartment. On Monday, Constance calls into work and leaves her manager a message that she is sick. Her doom is sealed when she hears the mailman at their box. She goes to the mailbox and finds an envelope with the words "From Tony to Constance." The letter inside reads:

Constance,
I have ended my lease. I told the landlord you are there. This month and next month's rent have already been paid. You have a little time to look for a roommate if you decide to stay. Rent is $1,200 a month. If you decide to leave now, this is a month-to-month lease, and the landlord said he would refund you most of next month's rent. Do not take any of the furniture; it came with the apartment.

Constance reads the letter and looks up into the air as she thinks to herself, That's why this place is so well coordinated. Then she returns to reading.

Make sure you do not allow anyone to take anything. I did a walk-through with the landlord and was cleared. Anything taken would be charged to you. The landlord will be in touch with you toward the end of your last month.
Happy life,
Tony.

The letter did not mention marriage or where he moved to. It is apparent to her that he has no intention of staying in touch with her, period. In her mind, he is gone—married and happy—and her churchgoing, prayers, and becoming a different person was a joke and have profited her nothing. She feels doomed.

After reading the letter, she calls back into work and speaks with her manager. She tells him she is weak and almost sure it is a virus but will get herself checked out. The manager believes her because he respects her work ethic. He tells her, "Four of my friends have had a virus, two were out for a week. One stayed out a couple of days and went back and made half of the people at their job sick. You take care of herself and get well. If you need a week, just call and let me know, because I don't want you to return too soon and end up getting worse or affecting others." She thanks him and hangs up the phone.

The conversation with her manager was bittersweet. Although they only have a work relationship, his response was typical for most men, one that was just what she wants, and she wonders how she failed so badly with Tony. She has no appetite and sits in the apartment, crying and staring at the walls.

By Monday night, she is weaker and desires to be free from the pain that has gripped her heart. She relives the restaurant conversation all night long. It plays in her mind like it is in a movie.

On Tuesday morning, at three o'clock, she lies in bed, staring at the ceiling. By four o'clock she is crying profusely; five minutes later, she stops crying, and for thirty minutes she tosses and turns. At a quarter to six, she draws up into a fetal position. Ten minutes later, she pulls the pillow over her head. She looks at her clock one last time and notices it is now a quarter past six. Finally she pulls the covers over head and lays in silence. Nothing helps her.

At eight o'clock on Tuesday morning, she sits on the side of her bed, wanting to forget about Tony and the conversation at the restaurant, but everything continues to play in her head nonstop. She has not bathed or brushed her teeth or combed her hair since Friday night, and she does not care. She has not watched television, listened to the radio, or spoken with anyone since she talked to her boss on Monday morning, and she does not care. She moves from her bed to a chair, back and forth, all day Tuesday.

Tuesday night at ten o'clock, she screams out in agony and falls on her knees out of exhaustion. She prays, "Lord, I don't know you. But here I am, a sinner, and I need you. I haven't been living for you or even trying to serve you. I'm everything I don't wanna be. I feel trapped. I don't wanna be like this. If I've caused anyone this kind of pain, I'm sorry. I can't blame anyone for the way I am but me. I … I … I want to change. I want to change, God! I want to know you. Oh, God. I need you. God, I need you. Please, God, help me."

After she stops praying, she stays in a kneeling position next to her bed and remains quiet. She falls asleep out of exhaustion on the floor. But as quickly as she falls asleep, she wakes again. She gets off the floor and lays across her bed in the pitch darkness of the room, looking up toward the ceiling. She isn't aware that she is taking shallow breaths that make her lethargic and weaker. She thinks about a character in a book she read that stated, "I am physically exhausted, mentally disturbed, financially depleted, socially ruined, economically outcast, and spiritually dead." She says, "That's me."

The time passes slowly. She gets up, walks over to Tony's old bedroom, and lies in his bed. Still in darkness, she stares at the ceiling, thinking, His room is no help; as much as I want to, I can't sleep.

She turns her head to the right side and finds herself staring at the clock radio. In the darkness, she reaches to turn it away from her so she cannot see the time—three o'clock—lit up on its face and accidentally hits the on switch.

A deep, soft male voice breaks the silence in the room and says, "If you are awake this morning, it's not by chance. I have a new song, entitled 'You Say.' Here it is."

The music begins, and the words cut through Constance to the bone. After hearing the first line, she was in tears.

You say you wanna serve him and live your life his way.
You say you wanna know him and never go astray.
But what I've seen is not what is coming through your voice,
and what I hear has not been the actions of your choice.
I beg of you to stop now and see just what you do.
Turn around and feel now what you put others through.
I beg of you to look up and know just what you say.
You're only safe when you set your sights on walking in his way.

That night is the first time Constance has felt a true desire for the God she has for so long convinced others she knew and loved. From her Bible reading to impress Tony, she has learned that wisdom calls for all to leave their simple ways behind and live. Until now, she has not been able to hear wisdom. But because of her brokenness, she hears wisdom speaking through the words of the song.

As she listens to the song, the words start to replace the restaurant conversation and her thoughts of Tony. The lyrics force her to see and think only about herself. She finally falls asleep, not waking until late afternoon. When she awakes, she calls her boss and tells him it is a virus, she has no appetite and has lost a lot of weight. He insists she give herself at least four more days to see if it runs its course.

For the rest of Wednesday, through Thursday, she mopes around the apartment, watching television, trying to get relief from the pain and heartache she feels. She cannot understand why she is not able to shake the fact that Tony is not for her. She begins to think she really must have been in love.

On Friday morning, she tells herself, "I feel better, and he doesn't matter." She has no appetite for food but eats a small bowl of cereal, cleans up the apartment, and decides to take a walk. She takes a long hot shower and washes her hair, and then she puts on her favorite jeans and T-shirt, walks over to her dresser, and fixes her hair. "I'm over it," she tells herself, then picks up some coins from a glass bowl on her dresser. "I feel like a Coke," she says as she places them in her pocket. She walks to her front door, opens it, and stands there for a moment, allowing the sun to shine on her face. She closes the door and walks slowly down the steps.

"This is just what I need," she says.

The landscaping around the apartment is beautiful. She stands on the steps for a moment and looks around. She walks out of the complex and strolls down the sidewalk. The street is quiet.

After walking four blocks away from her apartment complex she sees a car driving up the street toward her with a man and a woman in it. As they pass by, she sees their faces. They look happy. Another car comes by; the driver looks a lot like Tony. As that car passes her, she realizes it is not Tony. But by then, the sick feeling in her stomach has returned. She stops walking, stands, and screams at the top of her lungs. Then she looks around. There is no one there.

Tears roll down her cheeks, and she becomes furious with her mother. Now closer to the Convenient store that has a phone booth, rather than her apartment, she walks two additional blocks to a pay phone. With tears rolling down both cheeks and her hands trembling, she places coins in the slot and dials her mother's number.

June answers. "Hello?" she says.

"Ma, why did you make me like this?" Constance asks with a trembling voice, crying.

"You! Where's my book?" June asks.

"Why, Ma?"

"Make you like what? Where is my address book? You went in my room and stole it. What? You thought I wouldn't find out?"

"Forget the book," Constance screams. "Why did you do this to me? Can't you hear I'm hurting?"

"And you should be. I sent you to get rent money. I know you left to run to the family and tell my business. That's why you hurtin'. Thought they cared, didn't you? They don't care 'bout you. I told you: you need me, and I need you. But you didn't wanna be a part of this family, so you ran off. Sounds like you got just what you deserve for puttin' my business in the street," June says.

"This is not about you!' Constance yells.

"Then why did you take my book?"

"I'm hurting, Ma. Don't you care?" Constance asks.

"Yeah, I care. Now get back here, and bring my book with yo silly self. I told you, we just alike," June says.

"I'm not like you. You made me like this, and I'm not ever coming back!"

"You think I care?" June asks. "Just send me my book. You haven't learned anything."

Constance wipes the tears from her face and calms herself.

"You're wrong, Ma," she says. "I've learned a lot. I didn't tell yo business. Everybody already knows."

"Listen, you slut," June says.

"No, you listen," Constance says, her tears rolling again. "That's what you made me. But I'm much more than that. I'll show you."

"Constance, git me my book," June says.

Constance hangs up while June is still talking. She walks back to the apartment and calls work.

"Hello. It's a great day at Bargain World, Spree speaking, may I help you?"

"Spree?"

"Constance?"

"Yes, it's me. Is Mr. Michaels there?"

"No. Girl, Glenda quit last week; he has me helping out in the office. You sound awful. Are you okay?"

"Would you tell him I called? I'm not better yet."

"Sure. I hope you feel better."

"Me too."

"Since I started working at the front counter, I met this handsome hunk. I can't believe I hadn't seen him before."

Constance is silent. Uninterested, she says, "Yeah? I gotta go."

"I took advantage of the opportunity to drill that hunk. His first name is Baryy. That's Baryy with two 'Ys.'" Spree speaks in her proper voice. "Last name Greene."

Constance closes her eyes and shakes her head. "I gotta go."

"Sorry; Mr. Greene just, ooh, turns me on. I'll let Mr. Michaels know you called."

"Thanks," Constance says.

"No problem; get well, girl."

Constance hangs up, thinking, *Mr. Greene; where have I heard that name?*

Chapter 7
Modus Operandi

Baryy Greene is a professional womanizer and schemer. He has spent the greater part of his adult life looking for Ms. Right. In his mind, there has to be a woman out there who wants a handsome, loving man to share her wealth with. He has gone through women—which he calls his "casualties"—like sand runs through one's fingers. These casualties were all beautiful women: independent, self-sufficient, hard-working, and very successful. They possessed charm, charisma, and talent. So what's the problem?

The problem is Baryy; he doesn't just want a wonderful woman. He wants a wonderful woman who can afford to fund his business and enable him to live a lavish lifestyle ... a woman with no money issues at all. He wants a life where, if he wants to go to work on any given day, he will, and if he does not, he won't, and it's no problem because money is abundant.

Baryy is an extremely handsome man of medium height and muscular build with a slim waistline and neat appearance. He has met many women and has discarded them all. How does he do it? Baryy's modus operandi, or MO, is get to know them; make them feel safe and loved until they trust him; discover their true financial status; and assess whether it fits the profile. If not, he ends the relationship and moves on. So far no one has fit the profile, so he continues to move on. And in moving on, the first thing Baryy does is find a woman worth checking out.

At an early Sunday morning service in Jacksonville, Florida, people are hurriedly entering the sanctuary of a big church. The sun is slowly making its way across the church's parking lot as it warms the air. It is springtime, and everyone is dressed for the season. With smiles on their faces, they enter the vestibule and greet each other.

Baryy walks into the sanctuary, is greeted by an usher in the vestibule, and makes his way to the end seat of one of the middle pews. The pews fill up fast, and a beautiful young woman sits right next to Baryy. As she takes her seat, he notices she is not wearing a wedding ring.

"Good morning," he says.

Her eyes scan the pews several rows in front of her. Finally, she looks at Baryy and says, "Good morning. How are you?"

"Great," he says.

As she places her purse between her and Baryy, he asks, "Are you a member here?"

"No," she says. "I visit here often. Are you?"

"Yes, for about two months," Baryy says. "I really enjoy our service."

She smiles and says, "So do I."

He smiles back.

"Are you considering joining?" he asks.

"I don't know. Maybe," she says.

The service begins, and their conversation ends. Four ladies and two men walk to the center area of the church directly in front of the rostrum, holding microphones. They begin singing songs of praise. After the third song, one of the men says, "Let us pray; thank you, Lord, for another opportunity to enter your house and sing praises to your name. Speak to us today, Lord; bless us to leave here renewed through your preached word. We thank you for it now. In Jesus' name we pray. Amen." They slowly walk back to their seats, and the pastor ascends the rostrum.

In a deep voice, he begins, "Saints of God, you need to know today that the master is still seated on his throne with all power in his hand. Let's give him praise."

The congregation claps loudly.

He continues, "Our word today is taken from the Book of Ruth. For those of you who don't know, God speaks to everyone, everywhere, and if you are listening for his still small voice, you can always hear what he is saying to you. I pray to God that you listen today for what the Spirit is saying to you. Amen, church?"

"Amen," the congregation says.

"I want you to listen for God's purpose, provision, and promise from this book as the Holy Spirit ministers to your heart," the pastor instructs the congregation.

Baryy notices the young lady doesn't have a program. She opens her Bible, taking a pen and small pad of paper out of her purse. He hands her a program.

"I was given two," he says, smiling at her.

She reaches for the program and says, "Thank you," and gives him a warm smile.

Baryy opens his Bible and program, thinking, *She's classy; fancy purse, and a sexy voice.* He refocuses on the preacher.

"There was a severe famine in Israel, so severe that a man by the name of Elimelech took his wife Naomi and two sons, Mahlon and Kilion, to another country, just to make sure they would survive the famine. This man was a man, not just in gender but in character also."

The young lady starts writing. Baryy looks over and sees the words "a man should be one in gender and character."

The preacher elevates his voice, "He wanted to make sure his family was well provided for. He did not mind leaving all that he had to start over. Yes, he wanted the best for them.

"But before long, this man's wife, the mother of his children, found herself a widow and childless. Yes, I tell you, one day she felt blessed. She had a husband, two sons, and two daughters-in-law. And before long—say 'before long,' church."

"Before long," repeats the congregation, including the young lady. Baryy looks at her and says, "Before long." She looks at him and laughs. *Friendly,* he thinks to himself as he looks down and admires her legs. Again he returns his focus on the preaching.

"She was in a broken state," the pastor continues. "But God, who is all-knowing, all-wise, and all-good, had already provided her with someone that was God sent. This broken woman had her daughter-in-law Ruth. Now, as I said, she had two daughters-in-law. But we clearly come to see in Scripture, there was God purpose with this one. How do you know when there is God purpose? If you don't see it beforehand, you will know when his promise is revealed. And we'll get to it in a minute, where you will see what the women say to Naomi and what God does through Ruth."

The pastor continues to preach. Baryy is listening, and he notices this young lady sitting next to him is listening too. The pastor ends his sermon by saying, "And right here in the text, God reveals his purpose, his provision, and his promise. God knew he was going to bless Israel with a savior." The young lady writes "purpose, provision, and promise" on her program. Baryy does too. The preacher takes the microphone off its stand and walks to the left side of the pulpit, saying, "Ruth may have been a Moabite, but when she said to her mother-in-law, 'Your God will be my God,' our great God was fulfilling his purpose to bring the savior into the world.

"When God blessed Ruth with her new husband Boaz, his provision is clearly seen. Though she, like her mother-in-law, lost much, God provided so much more. Chapter four verse eleven tells us that the witnesses proclaimed of Ruth, 'The Lord make the woman that is come into thine house like Rachael and like Leah, which two did build the house of Israel.'"

He walks to the right side of the pulpit. Baryy notices the young lady is nodding and joins in with others who are clapping. When she stands up to applaud the preaching, Baryy remains seated and looks at her.

She sits and the preacher continues, "And as if that was not enough, God showed his promise of being able to take away your shame and your pain in Naomi. Chapter four verses thirteen to sixteen tell us Boaz and Ruth married and moved Naomi in to live with them. They had a son, and they allowed Naomi to take care of him as if he were her own. The neighbor women said to Naomi, 'There is a son born to Naomi.'

"Church, our great God blessed this family to bring forth the lineage of Jesus Christ our Lord and savior. It's right there in the text—chapter four verses eighteen to twenty-two—you can read about the family line of the savior." The preacher slows his speech, lowers his voice, and returns to the rostrum.

He wipes sweat from his brow and continues, "Now, think about your own life. Don't you know God has a purpose for you? Have you not seen God's provisions and promises manifest in your life? Give him praise for what he has already done and is going to do."

The young lady folds her program, places it in her purse, and sits her purse on top of her Bible between her and Baryy. Baryy folds his program, places it inside his Bible, and sets it next to her purse.

After the service, they walk out into the vestibule together.

Baryy starts their conversation again by saying, "By the way, my name is Baryy Greene." He reaches to shake her hand. She extends her hand to him.

"Terri, Terri Washington," she says.

Baryy resumes his charming smile and says, "Allow me to ask, are you married? Are you seeing someone? I'm asking because I would love to take you to breakfast, if you're interested."

"Not married, not dating," Terri says, still smiling. "But I have other obligations this morning."

Baryy drops his head to the side and says, "Okay. Can I get your number for a rain check?"

"Sure," she says. She takes the pad of blank paper and a pen out of her purse. She writes her number on a sheet of the paper, tears the paper out of the pad, and gives it to him.

As his eyes scan her number, he tells her, "I'm in transition right now. I just recently relocated here, and I'm staying with my friend, Buddy, until I find a place of my own. I like to respect his privacy, so I don't give out his number. Can I call you tonight?"

"Sure," she says. "I'm in bed by nine o'clock, so if you have not called by then …"

Baryy finishes her sentence, "Don't call." Baryy looks her in the eyes and says, "I'll call you tonight."

"Okay," she says. "Nice meeting you."

"You too," he says. He watches her as she walks away.

At eight that evening, Baryy calls Terri. They talk and laugh for an hour. That Sunday night is the beginning of their relationship. Baryy thinks he's found a sweet churchgoing woman who is probably praying to God to send her a husband.

After two months of lunch and dinner dates, nightly telephone calls, and a couple of gifts, Baryy is ready to make his move. One Monday evening, Baryy calls Terri.

"How was your day, baby?" he asks.

"Terrible," she says. "I feel like I'm getting a cold, and work was hectic."

"I'm going to pray for you. First, tell me about it."

Terri pours herself out to him as he listens quietly, never once interjecting a single word.

Terri finishes her sharing, and Baryy says, "I want you to play those worship CDs I gave you and clear your mind. Here's what you do: Take a hot bath and rest. Trust me in this. You're not going to feel bad anymore, tonight or tomorrow. Okay?"

"Okay," Terri says.

Baryy prays for Terri and tells her he loves her before hanging up the phone.

Terri is astonished when she awakes the next morning and realizes her cold symptoms are gone. At work that day, everything goes smoothly.

Baryy calls Terri around noon.

"Hey, baby," he says. "How's your day going?"

Her heart skips a beat as she says, "Just fine."

"That's all?" he asks. "Just fine?"

"Well, I must admit …"

Slowly, he says, "Yes?"

"I feel better," she says. "Like I never had cold symptoms. And work has not been hectic."

Baryy responds, as though his team has just won the playoffs, "All right! That's my girl, That's what I'm talking about. Did you bring those CDs to work with you so you can listen as you work and stay in this relaxed mood?"

"No," Terri answers reluctantly. "I left them home."

"No?" Baryy says, sounding let down. "You can't let your guard down with the enemy. You have to stay in a worship mode."

As glad as Terri is to hear his voice, she has something burning on her heart, and she wants to release it. She is silent for a minute, and then she breaks her silence, ignoring Baryy's statement about not letting her guard down.

"I wanted to call you this morning," she says, "but I couldn't since I don't have a number for you. You can always get in touch with me, but when I want to talk to you, I have to wait for you to call."

Baryy, a professional at thinking on his feet, says, "Baby, I told you, I like to respect my man's privacy. You know I'm working on getting my own place. I know what I want, and I haven't seen it yet. What's the matter? Don't you trust me?"

"All I know is that I have no idea where you live, who you live with, or when you're gonna call. But you know everything about me. You've been to my house and job."

Baryy thinks about his visit to Terri's home, which is a mansion.

"I'll tell you more about me tonight," Baryy says. "Meet me tonight at Finer Dining Restaurant on Kennedy Street at six thirty."

Baryy wants to make sure he charms Terri into being okay with not being able to call him. He realizes she must have awakened and felt so good that she wanted to call him immediately, and when she couldn't, it frustrated her. Baryy is confident he is well on his way to learning her financial status.

Baryy succeeds in getting Terri to forget about being mad at him. Her response goes from frustration to surprise as she thinks about the Finer Dining Restaurant.

"That's pretty upscale," she says.

And with the quickness of a stalking lion, Baryy replies, "Yes. And you're worth it. I'm your Boaz. Don't you know that?"

"No, I don't," she says.

Always ten steps ahead, Baryy says, "Well, you will. I have to go. I'll see you tonight, okay?"

At first, she is silent, just trying to take stock of her feelings and the conversation. Then she sighs like the prey that knows it's caught and says, "All right."

At six thirty that evening, Terri walks through the front entrance of Finer Dining, escorted by the host. She sees Baryy sitting in a booth on the right side of the room. The candles on the table cast a glow on his face. He smiles and waves to her. She smiles back and points in his direction. The host walks her over to Baryy's table.

"Enjoy your evening, sir and madam," he says. "Your waiter will be with you shortly."

Baryy stands up and pulls out Terri's chair. He notices her staring at his body. As she sits, he slowly pushes her chair closer to the table. He leans down and says, "Baby, I have something for you."

He hands her a tiny gift box. Terri looks at Baryy and then the tiny box, as he takes his seat.

"Baryy, you didn't have to," she says. "I just want you to be straight with me."

She sets the box on the table and does not open it.

Baryy takes her hand and says, in a deeper than normal voice, "I love you. I'm here for you. I'm not in your life by chance." He raises his brow and smiles. Then he says, "Let's enjoy our evening."

He stares deep into her eyes and kisses her hand and places the tiny box in her palm. She opens the box to find a beautiful bracelet made of diamonds and snow white pearls. "Oh Baryy, it's beautiful; thank you," she says in a soft voice.

The evening is relaxing and romantic and ends with Terri leaving Baryy at the restaurant. He does not tell her any more than she already knows about him. But Baryy knows Terri enjoyed the evening—so well that she did not want to spoil the moment. He does not know this because she told him, he knows this because he has been down this road so many times. He has learned the taste of victory and how to avoid unwanted conversations—the ones about his life, which he always refuses to have.

The next evening on the telephone, Baryy continues to charm Terri.

"Hey, baby," he says. "I didn't get a chance to call you at lunch today. How was your day?"

Terri gladly pours out her heart. "You won't believe what happened," she says. "I came home to water all over the kitchen floor. The pipes under the sink are leaking. On top of that, I went outside and locked myself out of the house. I've been outside for a while, trying to remember where I hid the key. I'm really just getting back inside now."

"Honey," Baryy says, "there is a shutoff valve under the sink."

"I know," she says. "The water is off. I went outside to get the mop and the door locked."

Baryy is silent. He can hear the tension, frustration, and aggravation in Terri's voice. She is just about to speak again, but Baryy says, "Now I have a question for you."

Frustrated because she is not in the mood for questions and does not understand how what she said can invoke a question, Terri snaps at him and says, "What?"

Baryy remains cool, calm, and collected. Gingerly, he says, "Are you going to continue to let me look for a place, or are you going to allow your Boaz to come and take care of you?"

Terri is completely caught off guard; she answers slowly and hesitantly and says, "I don't know."

Baryy flows in and out of smoothness, like the pro he is. His voice becomes stern and manly. "What's to know?" he asks. "Do you think we met by chance? I don't believe in luck. Baby, we were destined. I want to take care of you."

Terri is silent. Baryy knows he has her.

"Baby," he says. "I'll be there tomorrow after you get off from work. Once I'm settled, I'll take care of the pipes and everything else. Leave it all for me. Take a long, hot shower. I'll call you back. I love you."

Baryy hangs up. He calls back around nine o'clock and sings to Terri until she is too sleepy to stay on the phone.

Chapter 8
Smooth Operator

The next day, Baryy moves in. In one day, Baryy repairs the leaking pipes under Terri's kitchen sink and also does some other minor repairs. As live-in mates, the two of them get along well.

All Terri knows about Baryy is that he is a photographer. And since he is new in town, he has positioned himself with his church and several other churches in the area, so his name has gotten out as a professional photographer with reasonable prices. Between church members and local civic groups, he keeps himself very busy. She had worried that he might have other ladies in his life, but since he moved in with her, she now believes that he has nothing to hide.

What she does not know is that Baryy isn't interested in having several ladies in his life; he is hiding the fact that he really does not want to work. His ultimate goal is to marry a rich woman and have his photography business on the side. He is sure he can have what he wants and is both patient and determined to get it. With each new lady, he wonders if she is the one. So far, all past relationships have not yielded the lifestyle he is looking for.

He also knows that his most prosperous times are during spring, summer, and fall, when people are more interested in photography services. During winter, his income drops to almost nothing. He always works his plan to be a live-in mate with his new lady before winter. And as with his other friends in other cities, he needed to move in with Terri, because he has told Buddy he would only be staying with him for a couple of months.

For Baryy, friends come in handy when relocating and looking for a new love. As has been the case each time before now, when he assesses his new love's financial status, the relationship ends. He moves in with another of his buddies in a new city, and his chase starts again.

As with his other friends, he tells Buddy he will be out in a couple of months, and he is, because his plan with Terri works. He moves in with Terri just in time. Fall is over; winter has officially arrived.

On a wintry Friday evening, Baryy and Terri are enjoying a roaring fire and lounging on an oversize, leather sofa. Baryy is on one end of the sofa, and Terri is on the other. They are both quiet and staring at the blazing flames that are lighting and heating up the room. Smooth jazz is softly playing, making it a warm, cozy atmosphere.

"Foot massage?" Baryy asks.

"Oh yeah," Terri says.

They both sit up, and she props one foot on his lap. Baryy massages her foot and gazes into her eyes.

"I need to talk with you," he says. "I hate this. I don't even want to think about it."

Totally caught off guard and curious, Terri places the foot Baryy is massaging on the floor.

"What is it?" she asks.

Still looking in her eyes, Baryy opens up—knowing this is the one thing Terri has been waiting for him to do.

Baryy begins by saying, "Every spring, summer, and fall, I work like a dog to open my business. And every winter, work drops off so bad I can't get it off the ground. It's happened again this year. I hate it."

Internally, Terri breathes a sigh of relief. She had no idea what he was about to say. Now that he has spoken, she feels better and seeks to encourage him.

"Don't do this to yourself," she says. "Start small—hopefully, it will only be for a little while—and allow your business to grow." She thinks her words are loving and encouraging.

"Terri, you don't know what kind of man I am, do you? I try to show you who I am and what I'm about. I don't do anything small. If I'm going to do it, I am not going to hope it works out. I'm going to know it because I have the solid income to make it happen. Don't you see I'm standing on the wall for both of us? I'm a man who is the true head of the household, not just in gender."

Terri realizes her statement was not right for him. She sighs and looks away.

"Baby," Baryy asks her, "am I your Boaz?"

Terri looks at him and nods in affirmation, but she remains silent.

Baryy continues, "Don't make me any less, okay?"

Very softly, Terri says, "Okay."

"What's eating you?" Baryy asks her, trying to think one step ahead of her.

Terri inhales deeply. Then she exhales slowly and says, "You know Ruth had a part to play as well."

Baryy burst into a big smile; he knows he has her just where he wants her. "And what was her part?" he asks.

"To help her Boaz build upon his empire," she says. She stands up and smiles at Baryy as she speaks in an eloquent voice, reciting Scripture, "And all the people that were in the gate, and the elders, said, We are witnesses. The Lord make the woman that is come into thine house like Rachel and like Leah, which two did build the house of Israel: and do thou worthily in Ephratah, and be famous in Bethlehem: And let thy house be like the house of Pharez, whom Tamar bare unto Judah, of the seed which the Lord shall give thee of this young woman." *Ruth 4:11-12*

Baryy smiles big and says, "That's my girl. You've been reading."

Terri kneels next to him and says, "Yes. Don't worry. You just keep doing what you're doing. We'll be okay until spring rolls around again and things pick up for you. I predict this is your year."

Baryy kisses her cheek and says, "How did I get so blessed with you?"

Terri melts when he kisses her. "Do you really feel you're blessed?" she asks. "I used to wonder about you when we first—"

Baryy touches her lips, cutting her off. He leans forward and gently touches her chin.

He says softly, "Hey, I have no agenda, no schemes, no cons. I've been blessed with you. Now let's settle this once and for all. Have you been blessed with me?" Baryy looks her directly in the eye.

"Yes."

"Yes what?" Baryy asks.

"Yes, I've been blessed with you."

Baryy gives a nod of approval. They embrace. As Baryy holds her, she grips him tightly, making sure not to let go. He can sense the tension in her but is confident he doesn't need to concern himself with it, feeling she is just into him. But when he removes his arms from around her, she continues to hold him tightly. Baryy removes her arm from around him and looks at her with his eyebrows raised.

"I'm sorry," she says, "I slipped away for a moment."

"Where?"

"Oh, it's, it's nothing."

Baryy's look does not change.

"My aunt Charlotte is upset with me." Terri says.

Baryy's look still does not change.

"I don't want to talk about it."

"At least not with me." Baryy says.

Quickly she says, "No. No, it's not like that at all. It's just so complicated." She looks down.

"I specialize in complicated," he says.

She looks up at him. "My mother was the youngest of five siblings. She got pregnant with me, moved out at eighteen, and married my dad. He died when I was just a baby. After his death, Mom decided to move back here."

Baryy rubs the back of her right hand. "Was that bad?"

"No."

"But somebody didn't like it?"

"Yeah," Terri says slowly, looking at him. "Charlotte. She felt like mom was taking advantage of my grandparents and raising me for free."

Baryy is delighted that he is about to find out about her finances. "Your grandparents couldn't afford it?"

"Oh no; money wasn't an issue."

Baryy rubs her cheek. "Honey, what you're saying doesn't make any sense. Your mother was eighteen, a grieving widow, a new mom, and obviously with parents who could help her."

"Can we talk about this later? I just want to be held."

With what he had just heard, Terri was sounding more like the one for him. He wasn't certain, but felt confident he would know before long. He pulls her to him, places her head on his chest, and turns the lamp next to him, off.

The fire warms the room and bounces their silhouettes off the wall, giving the room a coziness fitting for relaxing. As Baryy holds Terri in his arms, he feels her body grow heavy as she falls asleep. He ponders how he'll approach her for more information. The weekend passes without any mention of their Friday night conversation. Baryy looks for any opportunity to start it up again. On Monday evening, he walks into the bedroom. Terri is sitting at the foot of the bed, holding an envelope. As she looks up, she jumps.

"Now that's not a good sign," he says.

"I didn't hear you come in," she explains.

"But I'm in the house. Of course I'm gonna walk in the room," he replies.

"Yeah. Of course," she says.

Still standing in the door, he says, "Let's finish our conversation."

Terri looks puzzled.

"The one we started Friday night. The reason why you're jumpy."

"Not now, Baryy."

"Now, Terri. It insults me that you think I can't help you."

"That's not how I feel."

"It's how I feel," he replies.

They look at each other.

"Okay, Baryy. You wanna know?"

"Talk to me," he says.

Terri sighs. "My mom got pregnant with me at eighteen. My grandparents wanted her to attend college; but that's not what she wanted." Baryy walks over to the bed and sits next to her. She continues, "Mom moved out and married my dad, but he died."

"What happened to him?"

"Mom says he fell asleep driving home one night. His truck went off the road and hit a tree. No one else was hurt but he died on impact."

Baryy listens quietly.

"My grandparents' health started failing around the same time. At least that's what Mom told me. She said she moved back into the house because her siblings were all away working on their careers."

"What are their names?" he asks her.

"Well, there's Charlotte. She's the oldest, then Tess, Walter, and Harry, in that order. Mom was the youngest."

Baryy nods. "Okay."

"Anyway, Mom and I never moved out. She always said to me, "Terri, we have to be here for your grandparents because no one else is. We will never leave them. No matter what.' Charlotte hated it. She wanted my grandparents to put Mom out."

"You and your mom took care of this place?" he asked.

"There was live-in help. But we were the only family in the house. My grands didn't agree with Charlotte; that caused a wedge between them. No matter how she tried to convince them Mom was using them, they wouldn't do it.

"When I was sixteen, Mom and I went to the fair, got on a ride that jerked us around, and got off laughing; everything seemed fine. We walked around, eating cotton candy and enjoying ourselves. Two hours later, when we were about to leave, she collapsed. I screamed at the top of my voice. Help came from everywhere. But she was dead."

"Did they do an autopsy?" he asks.

"Yeah, but it didn't reveal anything."

"What was the cause?"

"They said a weak heart. I was devastated."

"Baby, I'm so sorry," he says as he places his arms around her and pulls both of them back on the bed.

Laying on his chest, she continues, "So I became the only family here for my grandparents; they became my parents."

"Your aunts and uncles weren't around?"

"Everyone lived out of town except for Charlotte. They came home, but not a lot. When they were here, Charlotte would visit."

"So what's up with Charlotte now?" he asks, gently stroking her hair.

"She said Mom and I were added stress to her parents." Terri starts to cry, as she thinks about a visit she made to Charlotte:

* * *

On the Sunday she first met Baryy at church, Terri had visited Charlotte, hoping it would be the last time they would argue about her grandparents' will. In fact, this was the appointment that kept Terri from going to breakfast with Baryy.

On that Sunday afternoon, she made her way down the winding country roads to Charlotte's home and rang the doorbell.

When Charlotte saw Terri standing on the porch, she said in a very serious voice, "Terri, come in. I need to talk to you."

Terri opened the door and walked in with a big smile on her face; she said, "Anything for you, Auntie. What do you need?"

Charlotte paused for a moment to make sure she remained as calm as she could, and then she said, "I needed time to grieve the loss of my dear mother and then, so soon after, my father, or I would have called you sooner. Let me get right to the point. I need you to stop this lie. You're a liar and a cheat. I don't trust you as far as I can see you. I am warning you, when I get to the bottom of this will situation, you are going to pay."

Terri gasped. Then she pretended to cry and said, "I can't believe you're treating me this way. You saw Grandmother's signature. She would not want you to treat me like this."

Charlotte took a seat on her crushed velvet sofa and said, "Save it for someone who gives a damn. There is one of you in every family: a cutthroat con pretending to be sweet, innocent, and a Christian. Ha! May God have mercy on your sin sick soul."

Terri ran out of Charlotte's house.

* * *

Baryy wipes Terri's tears. "We don't have to ..."

Terri cuts him off, saying, "Yes, we do. You're right; you're always right. This is why I'm jumpy." She starts again. "Mom's death was so hard on me. My grandmother sent me to counseling. It helped a lot. I finished high school, started college, and graduated early. I was gonna continue living with them but Grandma insisted I get my own place."

"That's good," Baryy says.

"Yeah, but I still came by to visit her and Granddad almost daily. Their health had taken a turn for the worse."

"What were they dealing with?" he asks.

"What weren't they dealing with?" she replies.

"Oh, it was like that?"

"Yeah." Terri sighs again. She aggrandize her lie and continues, "Then one day, out of the blue, my grandmother called me over. I remember her two friends, deacons from her church, were visiting. She called me in her room and told me she changed her will. Said it was all going to me."

"All what?" Baryy asks, hardly able to wait for her response.

"Everything; everything they own, she said, was mine."

Baryy thinks for a moment. "So, whichever one of them outlived the other, you would own everything along with that one?" he deduces.

"Yeah," she says.

Baryy makes sure not to squeeze her but instead moves in for what he feels is his home run.

"Are your grands in a nursing home?"

"Oh no. Grandma died nine months ago, then granddad six months later."

Baryy thinks for a minute. "Right around the time I met you?"

"A couple of weeks before I met you. He was still here with the help when Grandma died. After he died, there was no need for me to keep the apartment so I moved back here. I let the help go, except for the yard man. He comes when I call. I've pretty much distanced myself from everyone."

"So that's why you were at my church?"

"I grew up in their church, but I can't go there. There's too many memories."

Baryy sits up at the foot of the bed and kisses her forehead. "Okay. I get it. Charlotte's upset, and Tess, Walter, and Harry are upset?" he asks.

"No. Just Charlotte. The others read the will and they're fine with it. Money is no issue for them. They have their own. So does Charlotte. She's the CEO of her own financial consulting firm."

"Baby, this is not complicated. I feel your pain. You've lost a lot. You don't deserve to be treated this way. But don't ever feel like you have to hold things inside for my sake. I cover you, remember?" He kisses her. "Tell you what, let's get some dinner and take this up later." Terri agrees.

Chapter 9
Scheming and Dreaming

A new day dawns, and winter's bitter cold has brought with it a freezing rain. Baryy rushes out of his car and into the Finer Dining restaurant. He shakes hands with the waiter; they have come to know each other very well. Baryy brings all his prospective clients to Finer Dining. "Your table awaits you," the waiter says as he walks Baryy over to the corner booth.

As Baryy waits for his client, he sees a woman he dated two years earlier, being escorted to a table by the host. *Tonya? What is she doing here?* he thinks to himself.

After she takes her seat, she looks over and sees Baryy looking at her. She changes her seat so that her back is to him. Baryy laughs and shakes his head. Ten minutes later, his client walks in and sees Baryy in the corner. He walks over, shakes Baryy's hand, and takes a seat.

The client wastes no time getting right to the point. "I'm planning my daughter's sweet sixteen birthday party. I'm sparing no expenses. I want it to be a party she'll always remember."

"I understand; I'll make the photos show a memorable occasion," says Baryy. "When where, and what time?"

Baryy and the father close out their meeting after ten minutes. They shake hands. Baryy waits until his client leaves and then walks over to Tonya's table. When she sees him, he says, "Well, hello; how are you?"

"Great, for someone who just moved to town. What about you?" she replies.

"I'm great too; take care."

Baryy walks away. He leaves the restaurant, runs through the rain to his car, and drives home. The rain pours harder as he drives up the driveway, parks, and gets out of his car. He makes his way to the front door. Once inside, Baryy hangs his raincoat and umbrella on the coat rack. He smiles as he thinks about running into what he calls, one of his past casualties. He thinks to himself, *Tonya, she said she just moved to town. Funny that we happened to be at the same restaurant. If I didn't know better, I would swear she tracked me down. Then she dared to look at me with contempt. Huh, she don't know, I care about her as much as I do a worn-out pair of shoes.*

He goes to the fireplace and starts a roaring fire as he continues thinking about meeting up with Tonya.

He thinks to himself, *My Terri, yeah. She will be with her Boaz and she ... what did she say? Help Boaz build his empire. And she doesn't know that I saw the will that she accidentally left on the kitchen counter. This house is hers and everything the grands owned. I wonder just what that may be? This just might be my wife, and with what I have laid on her, I'm sure to have my cake and eat it too. Ahhh!*

His hope is to get her to open up and reveal how much her late grands were worth. He is glad to be home and anxiously awaits Terri's arrival. When he hears her key unlock the door, he goes into the foyer to greet her.

"Baby," Baryy says, "I've been waiting on you. Where've you been?"

"I just came back from visiting Charlotte."

"How is she?" Baryy asks.

"Oh, she's fine," Terri says, "just business stuff". She thinks about this being the third time she has spoken with Charlotte regarding the will, and Charlotte has said, *"May God have mercy on your sin sick soul."* She continues, "I have done everything I know to do to help her understand, but ..."

Baryy finishes her sentence: "But she's envious and jealous."

She nods. "Yes."

"You can't let Satan steal what's yours," he says. "I got your back. I'll say I was with you when your grandmother changed it. I didn't sign anything, because you had enough witnesses there already. You did have witnesses, didn't you?"

"Yes," she lies, "but they were my grandmother's friends, the deacons, who died before Grandma."

Baryy laughs and smiles. "Baby, relax," he says. "There is no one coming back from the dead to help your uptight aunt." He holds her shoulders, looks in her eyes, and says, "There's nothing she can do to you. Nothing. Relax. Your grandmother made her decision. I see how important this is to you; is Charlotte the only one I need to talk to?"

Terri looks surprised. "You would do that for me?" she asks.

"Absolutely," Baryy responds quickly.

Terri touches his face and says, "I love you."

Baryy melts. "Baby, I've been praying that whenever you felt it, I would hear it and not a moment sooner," he says. "Please, say it again."

"I love you," she says. "I will arrange a meeting."

"You do that," he says. "I've got you covered from all attacks of the enemy."

They smile at each other.

Terri calls Charlotte, but her aunt does not answer.

* * *

For the next two weeks, Charlotte prays to God to show her the truth. Finally, she remembers that her mother loved her church's rose garden. She went there often with her mother to pray. On one occasion, her mother told her, "Daughter, this is where I spend most of my time communing with God. My life's worth is right here." As Charlotte sits in her home, thinking about her mother and how she communed with God, she takes on her mother's communing and begins to talk with God. She decides she will start visiting the rose garden at her mother's church.

That next Saturday morning, she drives down the long country road to her mother's church. She sits right where she and her mother sat when her mother first brought her there, next to a beautiful arrangement of red roses that gave beauty to an old statue of an angel.

On her third weekend visit, as with her prior two visits, she sits in silence, communing with God and staring at the statue. But this time, she notices the statue has a small door in the back of it. She has to look closely to see it, because the statue is rusted over from the weather. She tries to open it, but it is sealed with rust. She leaves it alone and goes home. All week, that statue stays on her mind.

The next weekend, she returns with some tools to pry open the door. After several attempts, she successfully gets it open, and to her blessed amazement, inside is a signed will, both of her parents' wedding rings, a large sum of cash, and an old Bible. Inside the Bible is a handwritten note that says:

My God is not dead, and he is not asleep. He is the sovereign lord who watches over all my affairs. To whoever finds this, my God moved on my heart to place this here for him to be glorified. How, I do not know.

Charlotte begins to cry and praise God. She knew in her heart that something was not right with Terri and her will. Charlotte opens the will and sees a signature, and, an 'X". Tears roll down her cheeks as she thinks about the two signatures on the will Terri presented to the family. She cries harder, realizing, her mother signed with a regular signature and her father signed his name by making the letter X. The will stated:

Being of sound mind and body, I, Mr. Robert Harrison, and I, Mrs. Sally Harrison, have signed into being our last will and testament.

At the bottom of the will, in small print, it reads:

If there is ever a will presented on my or my wife's behalf that is not signed by both of us, it is invalid.

Charlotte smiles.

"God, you and you alone have shown the truth," she says. Her joy is that she communed and waited on God, and he revealed the truth, not in her time but in his time. She knew in her heart that there had to be something else, somewhere, because Terri was not telling the truth.

Before Charlotte leaves the rose garden, she prays the same prayer her mother wrote on the note.

"My God is not dead, and he is not asleep. He is the sovereign lord who watches over all my affairs. Amen." She looks up towards heaven and says, "Father, glorify thyself. Amen."

She leaves the garden with the peace of God, knowing the Holy Spirit brought her there and is leading her in what to do next.

*   *   *

Six weeks after Charlotte and Terri's last conversation, Terri calls Charlotte to request another meeting. Terri is so happy that she no longer has to wonder how she is going to get Charlotte to go along with her scheme. Baryy has made everything so easy for her. She will be able to keep secrets from both him and Charlotte.

With absolute delight, Terri calls Charlotte.

"Hello, Auntie," she says.

With poise, Charlotte says, "Hello, Terri."

When Terri hears how pleasant Charlotte's voice is, she thinks it strange, because even though Charlotte has never been nasty to her when she has called, she has never been this nice. But Terri is too caught up in her plot to care.

"I know you don't want to talk to me," she says. "But I want to set everything right. I think I can do just that if you give me another chance. All I need is just a few minutes of your time."

"Really?" she asks.

"Yes," Terri says. "You and I both know Grandmother would not like for us to be anything but civil with each other. I want to make sure you know the truth from someone other than me. I'm bringing someone with me who can vouch for everything I've said."

Charlotte's voice sounds happy as she says, "The truth, huh? That would be great."

"Okay," Terri says, smiling.

"When do you want to meet?"

"Anytime that's good for you," Terri says.

"Let's meet next Saturday. I have a lot to do this week," Charlotte says.

Terri is elated. "Please call Tess, Harry, and Walter and have them come too."

"Okay. I'll see you then," she says.

That same night at the estate, Baryy and Terri discuss the telephone call. Terri is a little anxious about the meeting and wants to make sure everything will be perfect.

"Baryy, I talked with my aunt today," Terri says. "The meeting is set for next Saturday."

Baryy is making a sandwich and seems unconcerned about the meeting.

"Okay," he says. "Leave everything up to me."

His nonchalant response makes Terri more anxious. Irritated, she snaps at him.

"Baryy, we need to make sure we're on the same page," she says.

Baryy maintains his cool. He looks up from making his sandwich and says, "Who stood on the wall for you when you had problems at work?"

"You did."

"Who prayed over you when you were sick until you felt better?"

"You did."

"Who has been with you and for you, since we met?"

"Okay," she says. "You have, but—"

"No buts," he says sharply. "I got this. Just introduce me to her, and then you listen while I talk." He puts his sandwich together, and after a moment of silence, he continues, "You said your grandmother called you over and gave you the new will. The people who witnessed it are all deceased. Only God could have them speak now. Period."

He looks at her, takes a bite of his sandwich, and leaves the kitchen.

Saturday arrives. Terri drives Baryy to Charlotte's house. She speeds down the winding roads and sharp curves from the city into the country. Baryy notices her speeding, but he decides not to talk, so he remains silent and lets her drive recklessly.

They turn onto a long driveway that leads to a big, brick house. Terri and Baryy get out of the car and walk up the walkway and up the steps. As Terri rings the doorbell, she looks at Baryy.

Nervously, she tells him, "My aunt is very angry and bitter. Please don't react."

Baryy looks confidently at her and says, "Relax. Everything is going to be all right."

Charlotte opens the door. Terri smiles and greets her quickly.

"Hi, Auntie."

Charlotte also smiles.

"Come on in," she says. She leads them to her living room.

Terri introduces Baryy. "This is my special friend, Baryy Greene. Baryy, this is my aunt, Ms. Charlotte Harrison."

Baryy extends his hand to Charlotte.

"Hello, Ms. Harrison. It's nice to meet you."

Charlotte does not take his hand, but she nods her head at both of them and says, "Hello, Terri. Hello, Baryy. Welcome to my home."

Looking around, Terri says, "Where's the rest of the family? I thought everyone was going to be here."

Charlotte smiles and replies, "Everyone is here that needs to be here. They will come to you later."

"Auntie," she says. "I never told anyone this. You know, I was just as grieved as everyone else when Grandmother died and then Grandfather so soon after. I didn't want to mention Baryy, because I wasn't sure about our relationship." She looks at Baryy and says, "Baryy has asked me to marry him, and I have accepted."

Baryy almost chokes, but he contains himself. For a brief second, he looks in amazement at Terri. When he looks back at Charlotte, he catches her looking at him.

"Really?" Charlotte says, responding to Terri's announcement while still looking at Baryy.

Baryy quickly gathers himself and says, "Yes, Ms. Harrison. Terri tells me there's a problem with her grandparents' will. I went with Terri when your mother called and asked to see her. Your mother's friends, Mr. Thompson and Mr. Jones, were there also." Terri quickly looks at Baryy. She never told him the deacon's names. Charlottes notices Terri's expression. Baryy continues, "I remember because I talked with them for a while when your mother took Terri aside to talk with her.

"As I recall, these two gentlemen were your mother's prayer partners, and she wanted them to be witnesses to the new will."

Charlotte looks directly into Baryy's eyes and asks, "You were there when my mother handed Terri the new will?"

Baryy stands taller, pushes his chest out, and says, "Yes, ma'am, I was. I am so sorry for your loss."

Charlotte laughs as she says, "No need. My mother has visited me, and I am no longer lost." Terri and Baryy look at each other. Charlotte stops laughing and says, "So let me be perfectly clear: you and Terri were dating while Terri was helping my parents in their time of need. My mother called Terri over one day, you went with her, and you talked with Mr. Thompson and Mr. Jones while Terri and my mother went in the back room. Mother and Terri returned, and you know for a fact the will Terri presented to our family is my parents' will?"

"Yes, ma'am," Baryy emphatically says, with a serious face.

Charlotte looks at Terri and asks, "Terri?"

Terri moves one step toward Charlotte and says, "Auntie, it's true."

Charlotte holds up one hand to motion for Terri to stop.

"Okay," she says. Charlotte walks toward her front door and opens it. Then she turns to them. "Thank you both for coming," she says as she holds the door open.

In silence, Charlotte continues to hold the door open for Terri and Baryy, waiting for them to leave. Finally, Terri looks over at Baryy and then starts walking toward the door, with Baryy walking behind her. She stops at the door and stands in front of Charlotte, who is still holding the doorknob.

Terri looks her aunt in the eyes and says, "Auntie, are we okay?"

Charlotte says, "What is the last thing I have consistently said to you, each time you have visited my home?" Charlotte looks at Baryy, who is standing to the left of Terri, and says, "Baryy, it was nice meeting you."

Terri walks out the door, walking carefully down the steps. Baryy walks next to Terri and notices her demeanor. He does not dare say anything, because he knows Charlotte is watching and listening.

As they drive away, Baryy looks over at Terri with a confused look on his face. "What was she talking about?" he asks, referring to Charlotte's last statement to Terri.

"Nothing," she says. "I don't remember. She is acting weird. I'm worried about her." She keeps her eyes looking straight ahead on the road.

Baryy notices that Terri is driving just as recklessly leaving Charlotte's home as she did on the way, yet he says nothing. He allows her to drive however she pleases, and he remains silent.

Chapter 10
The Schemer Schemed

Baryy notices Terri has been restless since they returned from visiting Charlotte. For three days, she leaves for work earlier than usual and returns home later than normal.

On Thursday evening, she and Baryy have dinner together at home; she hardly says anything. He can tell she is preoccupied, only giving him one-word answers. He figures she will be okay if he allows her time to work through her feelings. In the past, he has always asked her how she felt and then proceeded to listen attentively to her. This was to work his plan and win her over.

I have her now, Baryy thinks to himself. *Now, I know her thoughts. She wants me to be her husband. And she is loaded. This estate has to be worth millions, and it's all hers. She'll be okay. I'm sure, within a week or so, she'll be all over me about planning our wedding.* Baryy is feeling on top of the world. It has been a long time coming, but he always believed that if he was patient and diligent, he would find his dream woman. Terri is her—beautiful and rich, sexy and rich, single and rich, rich and rich.

Barry walks through the house, noticing each room's décor; the antiques and paintings alone were worth a fortune. He doesn't touch anything or remove anything; he just wants to take stock of what he is marrying into. He is confident he will get to the value—bank accounts, investment portfolios, and the like—before the wedding. He is already planning how to avoid signing a prenuptial agreement.

On Thursday night, he wants to hold Terri and tell her how much he loves her, but she is still so distant. He goes to bed early and thinks to himself, *I'll lavish my love on her tomorrow.* Smiling and feeling on top of the world, Baryy drifts off to sleep.

On Friday morning, Terri rises early again and gets dressed for work. She picks up her purse and keys and goes out the side door into the garage. Although Baryy is still sleeping, he is familiar with the morning sounds and knows Terri is leaving for work.

When the garage door opens, she drives down the driveway and out of the iron gates. She turns left and goes an eighth of a mile down the road, drives up to a wooden gate, gets out of her car, and opens it. When she returns back to her car, she drives through the gate, stops again, and gets out of the car to close the gate. She hurries back to the car, drives one fourth of a mile down a dirt road, and pulls up to a wooden shed.

She parks her car and makes her way to the double-size door and opens it. Inside are three golf carts. She starts one, backs it out of the shed, gets off the cart long enough to close the shed door, and then drives the golf cart back to the house on a back road. She drives up to the house and enters the home. She stays on the opposite end of the house in a guest room, lying in bed and watching television, waiting for Baryy to leave. She falls asleep, and when she wakes, she looks at the clock on the wall and figures Baryy should be long gone by now.

She quietly exits the room, listening for any sounds of Baryy still being in the house. She makes her way to a small sitting room near her bedroom and looks out the window. When she sees his car is gone, she turns and goes to her bedroom. She packs her clothes, takes her suitcases down the stairs, drives the golf cart back to the wood shed, and drives her car back to the house. After she loads her suitcases in the car, she leaves town.

On Friday evening, Baryy pulls up to the front of the house through the iron gate. He doesn't see Terri's car, so he knows she has not made it home yet. He goes inside, walks straight to the den, turns on the television, and plops down on the sofa.

As soon as Terri arrives, he thinks to himself, *I'll take her out for dinner.*

He falls asleep on the couch while waiting for her.

Two hours later, the doorbell rings, waking Baryy up. A little startled, he gets up and walks to the door.

"Who is it?" Baryy asks.

"Duval County Police, sir. Open the door."

Baryy looks through the peephole and then opens the door. Two officers are standing in front of him.

"Can I help you officers with something?"

"Are you Baryy Greene?" the tall one asks.

"Yes." The two officers stare at a paper the tall one is holding. He continues, "Is there a Terri Washington here?"

Getting agitated, Baryy says, "Yes."

"Sir, we're told you and Ms. Washington are trespassing on private property and must leave immediately."

"What? This house belongs to Terri."

"No, sir. This house belongs to the estate of Mr. and Mrs. Harrison. Their estate overseer has asked that you vacate immediately."

Baryy is now looking back and forth at each officer.

"In the bitter cold of night? I have nowhere to go. We need to get to the bottom of this. Look, I was asleep on the couch. I'm sure Terri is home by now. Let me go and get her."

Baryy turns and starts toward the dining room, calling Terri's name. The police walk into the house. She is not in the dining room, so Baryy walks to their bedroom. The police follow him.

When he looks in their bedroom, the closets and dresser drawers are all open. He can clearly see that all her clothes are gone. Baryy is surprised at the empty closets and dressers. He looks back and sees the police looking as well.

"Look," Baryy says. "I don't know what's going on here, but I came in from a long day, sat down on the couch in the den, and fell asleep. When I left this morning, Terri was here and her clothes were here."

"You're trespassing on private property, and the person you say owns this home, her clothes are gone?" the tall policeman says.

"And you don't know where she is?" the other one asks.

Baryy grabs the back of his head.

"Yes."

"Sir, you're going to have to come down to the station with us."

Upset and confused, half laughing and angry but trying to maintain his composure, Baryy says, "Officers, I know this seems strange, but I'm telling you—I am not trespassing." He looks around in disgust and yells, "Terri! Where the hell are you?"

"Sir, don't make this difficult," the tall policeman says. "Let's go."

Totally humiliated, Baryy walks past the officers, out of Terri's bedroom and into the den. He picks up his coat and follows them outside to the police car.

They drive him to the Duval County Police Station, where he is passed over to a another policeman with a deep voice. The first two officers leave him in a small room and exit to brief the third policeman. Baryy can faintly hear them saying something about "suspicious" and "hiding something." The two policemen leave, and the third policeman enters the small room.

"Mr. Greene," he says, "the officers say you have chosen not to have an attorney."

"I don't need one," Baryy says.

"Sir, we need you to tell us where Ms. Washington is."

"I don't know. I haven't seen her since this morning."

"When's the last time you saw her?"

"I don't remember. We usually don't talk in the morning. I just remember her getting up to get dressed for work. I rolled over, looked at her, and then went back to sleep."

"And you don't know what time that was?" he asks.

"No," Baryy says.

"What time does she normally go to work?"

"She normally leaves at seven thirty."

"So, is it safe to say you last saw her at seven thirty this morning?"

"Yes."

"So why didn't you just say that?"

"I don't know," Baryy says.

"You don't know, or you don't want to incriminate yourself?"

"No," Baryy says. "I am not a criminal! I don't need an attorney, and I should not be here because I have not done anything wrong."

"Well, there's still the trespassing issue."

"I'm telling you, I live there with Terri!"

"Okay, you say you last saw her this morning at seven thirty and now have no idea where she is."

"Yes! That is exactly what I'm saying. Her clothes are gone. Doesn't that tell you something?"

"What is it supposed to tell me?" the officer asks.

"You people are impossible! I don't believe you!"

"I don't believe you realize how this looks. We are charging you with trespassing on private property. Now this is my last time asking, you have a right to an attorney. If you cannot afford one, one will be assigned to you."

"Who? One of your puppets? No, thank you," Baryy says.

Baryy is booked and placed in a holding cell.

A fourth policeman walks up to the cell and says, "You get to make one phone call, buddy."

Baryy is sitting on the cell's bunk bed with his head down and hands on his forehead. "I have no one to call," he says as he looks up.

The policeman walks away.

Ten minutes later, Baryy stands up, walks over to the bars, and yells in the direction of the desk. He sees the fourth policeman sitting at his desk, writing.

"Officer," he yells. "I need to ask you something, please."

The fourth policeman looks up from his writing and walks over to the cell.

Baryy clears his throat and says, "Please, just hear me out. I don't have anyone to call, but can you call the person who said I was trespassing? I don't have to talk with them, but will you please tell them I asked you to call? I really need you to do this for me."

The policeman stares at Baryy for a moment, says nothing, and then walks away.

Two hours later, Charlotte walks up to Baryy's cell.

Baryy looks up from sitting on his bed and quickly moves to the bars.

"I knew it was you," he says. "And I knew you would come. I could feel something about you the day I met you."

Charlotte stands in front of Baryy's cell with her purse on her right shoulder and her arms folded.

"You could feel something," she says, "yet you continued in your lie. Why?"

Baryy holds his face and says, "Ahhh, I was wrong. I was not there when your mother gave Terri that will."

"Oh, I knew that," Charlotte says quickly. "Neither was Terri; my mother never called her or gave her anything. If I had to guess, little Ms. Terri found the original will, and what she did with it, I don't know. But what she presented to the family was not the original.

"My parents had two wills witnessed. One they kept in their home, which Terri stole, and another one, I now have."

Baryy is shocked. "You?" he asks. In disgust, he lifts his face up toward the ceiling and place his hands on top of his head, then he says, "I knew it … It's like I knew everything you're telling me. I already knew."

Charlotte shakes her head at Baryy and asks, "If God has given you the spirit of discernment, why are you playing with his gift?"

Baryy stares at Charlotte. He grabs the bars and says, "I'm willing to be completely honest." He lowers his voice. "Just please, get me out of here."

"Oh no," Charlotte says. "If you are going to be honest with anyone, be honest with God. Only against God have you sinned and fallen short, and you don't need to be released to do that."

Baryy looks convinced. He is silent for a moment, and then he begins to talk.

"I met Terri over the end of spring heading into summer. We met at church. She gave me her number. We started talking. Soon, I convinced her to let me move in and take care of her."

Charlotte interrupts, "But you were just someone looking for a free ride. You're the type that uses women like they are old clothes—once new and worth the wear, but now they just don't suit your needs anymore. So you discard them for new ones. All you want is what you can get, at any cost."

Baryy looks at her in amazement, because he knows he was only in her presence for the few minutes he spent at her home.

"Yes. He gave it to me too," she says, referring to God's gift of discernment.

Baryy drops his head and says, "You knew—"

She cuts him off. "What? That you and Terri were lying?" she asks. "Yes. I know yall's kind. I told you both I was at peace; my mother had visited me; and they would be coming. Neither one of you was listening."

Baryy thinks back to the visit at Charlotte's home and says, "They ... the police?"

"Yes," Charlotte says. "When Terri called me to set the meeting, I knew everything I needed to know. Terri's fake will had both my parents' signatures, but only my mother signed their will."

"I think Terri found my parent's will by snooping through their personal belongings when she was supposed to be helping them. She did not have enough sense to realize they both signed the will. My father, who at the time could no longer write because of his tremors, was only able to sign by marking the letter *X*. I'm sure Terri looked at the will long enough to assume that the *X* represented where my mother was to sign, because my mother's signature was right next to it. She didn't even bother to read the small print at the bottom of the will, or she would have known how my father signed the will and that my parents had two originals".

"I prayed that Terri would end this lie and repent before God. That's why I set the meeting for the end of the week."

She reaches into her purse and pulls out her keys. Then she shifts her purse to the other arm as though she is getting ready to leave.

"And now, here you are," she continues. "What are you going to do?"

Baryy grips the bars and mashes his face into them.

"You know I didn't have anything to do with Terri's forgery. Please, tell them that," he says, moving his head in the direction of the officer's desk.

"Your case needs to be presented to the Lord," Charlotte says. "I will not get involved in what he is doing in you."

She walks a couple of steps away from the cell and then turns and looks back toward Baryy. He doesn't want her to go. He feels alone. He knows she is about to speak and hopes her turning means his release; he wants it badly. But instead she tells him, "Your being in jail is a luxury compared to the jail your soul lives in. Repent".

"When you do get out, if I may suggest, there is a beautiful rose garden at Pilgrim's Rest Church on Eighth Street. In the garden, there is an old angel statue with beautiful roses planted around it. You can find a sweet place to commune with God, who is not dead and is not asleep. He is the sovereign lord who watches over all your affairs."

Charlotte leaves.

***

That same night after Charlotte leaves, Baryy sits in silence in dim lighting on his cell's bunk bed. He is so still, like he has been mummified. After a few minutes, he looks around the place looking at each empty cell. No one is there except for him.

He can hear two officers talking and a radio playing. He hears one officer say good night, and a door closes. The place becomes quiet. It is as if he is the only one there.

He hears a deep voice on the radio say, "Wherever you are out there, listen and consider. This is a new track entitled, 'You Say.'"

Then the officer picks up the phone and starts a conversation. After he hangs up, Baryy hears these words from the song on radio:

You say you have no agenda, no need to lie at all;
you say you're in his purpose; a watchman on his wall;
you only speak for Jesus; you only live for him;
but ask yourself have you been his representative.
I beg of you to stop, now, the things you do and say.
For someone of your caliber, your life shouldn't go this way.
I beg of you to stop, now, the things you talk about.
For someone who says you love the Lord, your time is running out.

The cell's dim lighting goes out. The only light remaining is a night-light shining into his cell from the hallway. Baryy can see his shadow on the wall.

He feels humiliated and wants nothing more than for this to be a bad dream. As each minute passes, his emotions range from humiliated to hurt to angry to lonely. He becomes so deeply distressed, he cries out, "God!" Then he is quiet for a long while, just staring at the wall and faintly breathing. He does not even move.

After a few moments of stillness, he drops to his knees on the side of the bunk bed and prays, *"God, I know you're real. I know nothing about praying to you. But I do know I'm tired. I thought I was strong, smart, and able to take care of myself. I feel like nothing. Please help me get out of this jail. God, you know this is the last place I want to be. I repent of all my sins; I forgive Terri. Please Lord, forgive me."*

After his prayer, he continues to say, "God, please forgive me."

Baryy understood God's message coming through the radio. He spends the next three nights in jail thinking, *I'm Baryy Greene. These types of things don't happen to me. How can I ask Buddy to bail me out without telling him anything? Surely, he'll want to know. If I just had someone to withdraw money from my bank account instead of involving Buddy.*

All my life, I've prided myself on being independent and closemouthed about my personal business. It's just common sense to leave everyone of out your business and definitely your bank account. Except for now. I wish I had someone on my account who could wire me money, then Buddy would never have to know. It's not smart to have a bank account with just your name on it.

Oh man, I don't want Buddy in my business. The only Baryy my friends know is the professional one. I want to keep it that way. I can't believe this. This is never going to happen to me again. But to get out of here, I have to start being honest and truthful. Buddy is going to know that I run women, and worse yet, this one made a fool of me.

On his fourth day in jail, Baryy sucks up his pride and calls Buddy.

Just as Baryy suspected, Buddy comes. He walks up to the cell and sees Baryy sitting on his cot. Buddy says, "Man, what are you doing in here?"

Baryy look up from his cot and says, "Cops came to the crib sayin Terri and I are trespassing on private property."

Buddy frowns. "What?"

Baryy stands up and walks to the cell bars. "I don't know if I can explain this to you."

Buddy stands tall. "Try hard."

"I know I told you I had my own place; I lied. I convinced Terri to let me move in her grandparents' mansion with her. I told you I was going to break it off cause she was gettin too serious. I lied. We were doing great; everything was cool. Three days ago, I came home from work and fell asleep on the couch waiting for Terri. Then the cops came."

Buddy stretches his brow. "You been in here three days?"

"Yeah, man, I didn't wanna call you; just hear me out. The cops woke me that night sayin' we were trespassing on private property and had to vacate. I told them to hold on and let me get Terri to straighten things out. I looked in the kitchen, den, bedroom; she wasn't there."

"What do you mean she wasn't there?"

"I don't know, man; she wasn't there. The cops followed me all through the house to the bedroom, and we saw all her clothes were gone."

"She packed her clothes; you didn't know, now she's gone. All in one day?"

"Yes. No. I don't know when she packed. I came in Friday, stop at the couch, and fell asleep. I thought she may have come in and just didn't wake me."

"Huh. Maybe y'all not so cool."

Baryy raises his voice, "I've thought about this over and over again. This is insane."

Buddy walks closer to the cell bars and lowers his voice. "Where is Terri?"

"I swear, man, I don't know."

Buddy backs up and says, "I can't get you outta here; I'm not gettin involved."

Baryy grabs the cell bars and stares at Buddy. "What? Come on, man; I wouldn't lie to you about this."

Buddy yells, "Your whole life is a lie!"

Baryy drops his head. "Somebody may be tryin' to set me up."

"No. You set you up."

"Okay. I'll take that, but I'm tellin' you, she was talkin' about marriage."

Buddy laughs.

"I swear; you know me."

"I thought I did."

"I run women. But I've never even raised my hand to hit one." Baryy is silent for a moment. "I've gotta get outta here to find out what's going on and where she is. I'm worried too. Come on, man; I can pay you back in full. I just need you to get me out."

Buddy looks Baryy in the eyes. "This better not be some crap you're laying on me, or I'll have you arrested myself."

He bails Baryy out and tells him he can move back in with him. Buddy drives Baryy from the jail house, escorted by the police, to meet Charlotte at the mansion and gather his belongings. He packs quickly without saying a word to Charlotte. When he finishes, he walks out to Buddy's truck and loads his luggage bags in the back. He musters up enough decency to thank Charlotte before Buddy drives him away. At Buddy's, he hurriedly unpacks and tells Buddy he's going to lay down for a while. When he closes the door to his room, Buddy yells to him from the hallway, "Hey man, I'm going out."

He hears the front door close. The house is silent. Anger raises up in him. He picks up his house key and walks out the front door, thinking, *This can't be real; I have to be in a bad dream.* He walks several blocks to the same grocery store where Constance and Spree work. The two women are there when Baryy walks in. Spree looks at Constance from her register.

"Hey," Spree whispers to Constance, "I know you thought I was lying, but that's him," moving her head toward Baryy, but the magazine rack blocks Constance's view of him.

"Who?" Constance asks, standing at her register, looking back over her shoulder.

"Baryy," Spree says, "with two 'Ys.'"

Constance looks back at Spree and shrugs her shoulders, as if to say, I still don't remember what you're talking about.

"Mr. Greene," Spree says with her lips tight. "The one who turns me on."

Constance looks back at the man. He moves into view. She sees him from behind. She says too softly for Spree to hear, "I remember that body."

"You see him now?" Spree says.

Constance nods, still looking at Baryy.

They each watch him disappear down the aisle. Spree wants to talk but they each have a customer. A couple of minutes later, he reappears in Constance's view from the far end of the store, heading toward the registers. She looks at him, thinking, *in Atlanta, I boarded the plane to Jacksonville behind you. So this is how the front of you looks.*

He notices her. Spree looks over at Constance and follows her eyes until she is now staring at him. Aware of them both, he chooses an older lady's register to check out, at least four registers away from them. He gets his change, picks up his beer and magazine, and walks by Spree and Constance.

Spree stares like a lioness who has spotted her meal. Constance sees a handsome man, but her heart is still cut open and bleeding. He does not look at them but walks to the door, thinking, *No. And even if you were my type, I don't need the cops thinking I killed Terri for her money and now I'm with you.*

The automatic doors open. He walks outside, where two men are shaking hands; he hears one say, "Okay, Staten; good seeing you, man."

"You too," the man says, backing up to enter the store. He bumps Baryy's shoulder. "Excuse me," he says.

"No problem," Baryy replies as he continues walking, thinking, *Staten? His face looks familiar ...*

Chapter 11
Quasi Pastor

In Canada, Bishop Hinson and a newly ordained pastor are scheduled to discuss the new pastor's assignment. The new pastor's name is Ralph Henley; he is thirty minutes early for his appointment. He reads a magazine while he waits.

When it is time, the bishop's secretary calls his name and escorts him into the bishop's office.

"Hello, sir," Ralph greets him. "I am so delighted to have been selected to lead the church in Jacksonville, Florida. Thanks for speaking up for me. I will not let you down."

The bishop smiles as he hands Ralph the envelope, containing Ralph's selection letter, sent to him, by his colleague, Bishop Carmichael, in Florida. He looks at Ralph and says, "You will not let God down, son. Carmichael and I agree that you will do a good job. I realize they have only heard of you, but that may be best for you and them. Everyone gets to let their light shine and to meet the true person within. Go and be blessed."

Ralph accepts the letter, holds it in his hand, and smiles at the envelope. He turns to leave the bishop's office.

When gets to the door, he turns, looks at the bishop, and says, "I'll be in touch; it may be a while, but I will be in touch."

"Carmichael and I are leaving for China at the end of the week," the bishop says. "I'll be gone for a while. Yes, we'll be in touch."

Ralph closes the door to bishop's office, stands in the hallway right outside the door, and places the envelope in his right, inside lapel pocket. Just as soon as he slides the envelope into the right lapel pocket, he quickly pulls it out and slides it in the left lapel pocket and walks away. He makes his way home, where all his clothes are packed in luggage bags and the house is empty with a "Sold" sign in the yard. He loads his luggage bags into his car, locks the front door, and places the key in the mailbox. He opens his car door and looks at the house, smiling. He gets in, starts the car, and drives away.

As Ralph drives south on highway 16 in Ottawa, Canada, he sings along with a CD of praise songs and enjoys the thought of being a pastor and leading a flock. As he drives down a narrow mountain road, he sees an oncoming vehicle that has come out of nowhere and is traveling in his lane. When his eyes and brain comprehend what is happening, he tries to move into the opposite lane, but he cannot avoid the head-on collision.

The cars collide. Ralph is thrown from his car and is lying in a pool of his blood on the side of the road.

* * *

Vonder Staten's car is close enough so he clearly witnesses the accident. When he sees the two cars collide, Vonder immediately slows down, pulls over to the side of the road, and parks. He gets out of his car and makes his way to the driver closest to him.

As Vonder approaches the driver, he notices it is a man. He wonders to himself, *Why were you driving on the wrong side of the road?* He notices the man is not breathing. *He must have died on impact,* Vonder thinks. He decides to feel for a pulse anyway.

While feeling vainly for a pulse, he hears the other driver's faint groans and walks over to him.

"Sir," Vonder says, "can you hear me? Don't move. I'm calling for help now."

Vonder runs back to his car, opens the door, and reaches for his cell phone. He quickly dials 911. The operator answers.

He shouts into the phone, "Hello. I'm on Highway 16 , and there's been a terrible accident. We are right on the shoulder near mile marker 75, please hurry!"

After speaking these words, he runs back to the driver.

Vonder kneels down and looks at the driver's bloody face. The driver continues to moan and mumble in a faint voice, as he lies on the ground in a pool of his blood. Finally, Vonder moves his ear as close to the driver's mouth as possible to make out what the man is trying to say.

He hears the driver say, in a faint voice, "God help me. What about the flock?"

Vonder raises his head and looks in the driver's eyes.

"Flock? Help is on the way. What's your name? Is there someone I can call?" Vonder finds himself eye-to-eye with the driver. His watery eyes seem to pierce directly into Vonder's eyes.

"Pocket, poc-ket," the driver says in a faint voice. "Take it. This is for you."

The driver fades out of consciousness. He closes his eyes and says nothing else. In shock and confusion, Vonder watches helplessly as the man stops breathing.

"I have watched this man die," he says out loud. He then remembers that the man said, "Pocket," and "Take it."

He reaches into the driver's left coat pocket and pulls out an envelope and opens it.

Vonder reads:

Dear saints of God,

It is through much prayer and toiling that I have heard from the Holy Spirit and am sending you Mr. Ralph Henley to lead you. He has labored in God's vineyard for a while. Receive him now and be blessed.

Vonder continues to read the letter, which gives details of Mr. Henley's appointment as pastor of a church located in Jacksonville, Florida. He notices the letter was signed by Bishop Carmichael .

As he waits for what seems like forever for the paramedics, he stares at both bodies and reads the letter over and over again. He wonders, *What just happened here? Am I in a bad dream? Why is this happening to me?*

Vonder was raised in the church and believes in God, but he has never dedicated his life to Christ. He rarely attends church and never thinks about praying to God to know God's will for his life. Yet, he thinks to himself and decides, *This is not a chance happening. I know God is real. God is speaking to me. This man's last words were "Pocket. Take it. This is for you."* Vonder's thoughts carry him right where he wants to go: *God wants me to have this; there were many who were not learned and God used them mightily; so it is with me.* These thoughts grow and grow by the minute.

When the paramedics finally arrive, Vonder has transformed himself for the man's life and calling, not knowing or caring about what lies ahead. He tells the paramedics as much as he knows. When they are done with him, he leaves to start his new life.

* * *

Vonder arrives in Jacksonville and heads to the church to meet with the deacons.

Upon entering the church's main entrance, Vonder is welcomed by a church administrator, who directs him to the pastoral office.

Vonder walks to the office and knocks; a voice says, "Come in." He opens the door and walks in. Three deacons are in the room.

"We've been looking forward to your coming for months," one deacon says.

"Almost a year," another one interjects.

"How was your trip?" the third one asks.

Vonder shakes all three men's hands and then says, "Gentlemen, I'm Pastor Vonder Staten." They each shake his hand and give their name: William Albright, Tim Hines, and Greg Aims. Vonder continues, "I have some terrible news. Your new pastor, Mr. Ralph Henley, was in a terrible car accident and died tragically at the scene."

"What happened?" Aims asks.

"All I know is that I witnessed his car's head-on collision with another car," Vonder says. "The other driver was on the wrong side of the road. I think the driver must have fallen asleep, and Mr. Henley did not see him in time to avoid his vehicle."

"I don't know what to say," Albright says. "A man is called by God to lead his flock. He serves his time tarrying in God's word and is making his way to his place of service and dies on the way."

"No man knows the mind of God," Aims says. "We need to pray for understanding."

Vonder looks at Aims and says, "I think I can help you understand. Maybe what Mr. Henley said to me will make sense to you as it did to me."

"What did he say?" Hines asks.

"In his dying moments," Vonder says, "his last words to me were 'Pocket. Take it. This is for you.' He breathed his last breath and died."

Vonder pulls out the bishop's letter from his briefcase and hands it to Albright.

Albright reads the letter aloud, "Dear saints of God, It is through much prayer and toiling that I have heard from the Holy Spirit and am sending you Mr. Ralph Henley to lead you. He has labored in God's vineyard for a while. Receive him now and be blessed. Bishop Carmichael ."

After the letter is read, Aims says, "Again I say, no man knows the mind of God. We need to pray."

Albright ignores Aims. Shaking his head in disbelief and dismay, he says, "We have a hurting congregation awaiting their God-appointed spiritual leader.

God is not a God of confusion. He chose to take one son and send another. I say we welcome this pastor."

Hines agrees with an "Amen." Then he reaches out his hand again to receive Vonder with a handshake.

Albright extends his hand while saying, "Welcome aboard, Pastor Staten."

Aims walks toward Vonder and asks, "Where did you receive your training?"

Before Vonder can answer, Albright pulls Vonder further away from Aims and says, "From God! We'll get all his information, but now, we have sick people to visit, and he needs to get prepared for Sunday service." He pulls Vonder toward the office door. While hurrying Vonder out of the pastoral office, Albright says, "I'm sorry about that. Aims is old-fashioned. He always wants to wait. I tell you, Jesus will return on a cloud, and there would be nothing done if we did things his way."

Albright and Vonder walk to Albright's black Crown Victoria.

As they drive away, Albright says, "I am not expecting you to do anything but allow the sick to see you. We have some terminally ill members who just want to see the man of God."

They visit three members before Albright returns Vonder to his car in the church parking lot.

Chapter 12
Turmoil

The congregation loves Vonder. There are only a few who really have reservations about him, just like Aims. But their voices are not strong enough in the church to make a difference. These few decide to do what all true Christians do—stay watchful and prayerful while they wait to hear from God. Interestingly, these few church members feel the same way Aims feels, even though they haven't had any conversations with Aims, nor have Aims, Albright or Hines shared any part of their initial conversation with Vonder. These few members and Aims are independently and quietly praying for God's holy revelation and truth.

Three months later, the church congregation is growing. The church's financial situation has improved tremendously. Pastor Staten has settled into his new position. For the most part, the flock is hanging onto his every word, and all seems well.

Church growth is phenomenal. The pews have more people each month. People are excitedly involved in Sunday service, and a pastor's aid committee has formed.

The faithful few with reservations are getting more and more concerned as the congregation grows, the money pours in, and Pastor Staten's popularity reaches an all-time high. These faithful few are still praying and waiting for God to reveal his truth about how this pastor has come to be. All they see is a well-rehearsed showman with good showmanship.

One year to the day after Vonder's first sermon, Aims arrives at church extra early and makes his way to the meditation room. He kneels in prayer and stays there until he hears the service starting. He makes his way into the sanctuary to join in the praise and worship.

After praise and worship is over, he makes his way to the podium on the floor and taps the microphone to get everyone's attention.

"Good morning," he says. "Let us once again stand and give thanks and praise to God for another day."

The congregation stands, and they all clap their hands.

He gives them permission to be seated and says, "Please allow me to have your attention until I have completed what I'm about to say. I have some bad news. Our pastor was rushed to the ER last night. They are not sure what is wrong at this time. Deacons Albright and Hines are with him.

"The pastor has asked that we carry on with the service and give God awesome praise and honor that God may hear from heaven and restore him. And for those of you who are wondering, it was the pastor's specific request that praise and worship go up to God before any mention of his situation.

"He cannot have any visitors at this time. We will keep you posted." Aims pauses and then says, "And allow me to say from my heart, please pray as God leads you, not as you think you ought to pray."

Albright enters the church just in time to hear Aims speak from his heart. As service continues and the choir sings loudly, Albright sternly ask Aims if he can speak with him over in a corner of the church.

Both men walk to the back corner of the room.

"I can't believe what I just heard," Albright says in a low, stern voice. "Staten has brought this church from nothing, and he is lying in a hospital bed, gravely sick, with the doctors telling him they don't know what's wrong, and you are still doubting him a year later, after all he has done?"

"It is never wrong to pray from your heart as God leads you to do," Aims says with the same stern voice. "Man, who is your God?"

Albright places both of his hands in his pants pockets, as though he needs to keep from using hand gestures, and says, "Don't you dare judge me. I know God for myself. That man was sent here by God, and all you've done is treat him like a criminal."

With eyebrows raised, Aims says, "No. All I've done is pray to the Lord God Jehovah to show truth, and *that* I will never cease to do, no matter what! I will say this, I know something is not right, and God will reveal."

The congregation prays, fasts, and confesses, and nothing changes about Vonder's condition. Three weeks pass, and doctors still don't know why he is slowly deteriorating.

Vonder lies in his hospital bed every night, unable to sleep, worried sick about his health. *How can I be healthy one day and gravely sick the next?* he wonders to himself. *Do the doctors know and they just don't want to tell me? Am I dying? I know the saints are praying. I've prayed for many, and they have returned to church, sometimes in less than a week, rejoicing about their deliverance. Well, Aims and I prayed.*

Three weeks turn into six, and six turn into twelve. The doctors are finally saying they think it is a rare blood disorder.

Vonder is worried about the congregation. He sensed something was wrong and he could not have been more on point: the congregation is growing weary in their praying. All sorts of gossip has started. Many things the church members did not know, nor were ever supposed to know, are starting to come out, because Albright, disgusted with Aims, shared his feelings with Hines at the church one evening, and the receptionist overheard him. Albright falsely accuses Aims of calling Vonder a fake and of saying he was not sent by God to lead the church but one who came in his place, because the real servant died in a tragic car accident. The receptionist hears everything; once she hears, the gossip starts.

The gossip spreads like a wildfire from the receptionist's office throughout all the ministries of the church. From there, the gossip makes its way to the hair salons and barbershops. Church members are debating. Some say, "This is not the pastor that God sent but one who came in his place." Others say, "God did send him, because he decided to take the other one." This gossip goes back and forth between church members daily. This gossip is heard in the grocery stores, day care centers, and at members' jobs, until it reaches all the way back to the church meetings, choir rehearsals, and ushers' meetings. There is not an entity of the church that is spared from the gossip.

The members are split down the middle. Some believe the pastor is God's called pastor for their church. Others believe he is not. Those who oppose the pastor and his advocates are conversing.

"He has no formal training."

"God is the master trainer. Plus, one who is called needs no paper from man."

"Not all church growth is of God."

"The manifestation of the growth of this church and our finances says that God is on our side."

"God will allow man to set his own trap. God gives man much time to repent and turn from his sinful ways."

"All these people coming into the church ... That alone speaks of God."

"People are just hungry for someone to follow. And if that someone looks or sounds good, people will follow."

"You are just jealous and envious of the anointing on this man."

This gossip changes the church into a debating parlor, and true worship is lost.

* * *

Sinking deeper into sorrow and still in the hospital, Vonder makes a telephone call from his hospital bed, asking Aims to visit him alone.

Within hours of the call, Vonder looks up, and Aims is walking into his room.

"Aims," Vonder says, "thanks for coming. I really need to talk with you."

Aims pulls up a chair next to Vonder's bed.

"How can I help?" Aims asks.

"I'm dying. I know I am. Please, tell me. What's in your heart?" Vonder says.

"You are not called to be a pastor," Aims says. "You have no idea what God has called you to do. Do you?"

"I told you about the letter," Vonder says. "I thought God was speaking to me."

"You *thought*?" Aims asks. "Son, God speaks today just as he did yesterday and will do forever. If you really want to hear from God, he will speak to you."

Aims prays for Vonder and then turns to leave. He opens the door, looks back at Vonder, and says, "Son, be blessed."

That night, Vonder's mind goes back to the accident. He also thinks much about his life prior to moving to Jacksonville. He thought about the guys he worked with at the construction company and how they all would laugh and tell jokes to take the edge off of the grueling long days of intense work with loud machines. He knew he never really had any desire to get to know or serve God until the accident. The more he thinks, the more he seeks God in prayer, asking for help in his situation. The Holy Spirit leads him to find out more about the accident and just who Pastor Henley was.

The next morning, Vonder calls for Albright to visit him.

Albright walks into Vonder's room with a big smile on his face.

"How are you today?"

Fumbling with his hands, Vonder looks up at Albright entering his room and says, "I need you to do me a favor. Please keep this confidential."

Albright assures Vonder, "I won't say a word. Anything you need, just ask."

"I need you to get me as much information about the accident and Pastor Henley as you possibly can," Vonder says.

Albright sighs, places his hands in his pockets, and stands tall.

"You don't need to worry about a dead man. You're gonna live. Has Aims been here? That man is crazy," Albright says.

Vonder shakes his head frantically, saying, "Please! This has nothing to do with Aims. I need you to do this for me."

Albright says, "Okay. The congregation is praying, and they want to see you. What should I tell them?"

Vonder settles down from his anxiety and says, "Tell them that God will speak to me. And I will speak to them. Until then, keep praying."

Albright nods in affirmation and leaves.

In less than four days, Albright delivers the information to Vonder, who then asks Aims to come see him again.

Aims hurries to Vonder's hospital room.

Their conversation is right to the point.

"Thanks for coming," Vonder says.

"How can I help you?" Aims asks.

Vonder points to a folder at the foot of his bed stuffed with sheets of paper and a newspaper article.

"I asked Albright to gather all this information for me," he says. "He doesn't know why. I just asked him to get it. He doesn't know I have called for you, and I don't want him to know—at least not yet."

Aims looks at the folder and asks again, "Why have you called for me?"

"Because I know God is with you," Vonder says, "and if I'm going to get the answers I'm seeking, I need someone who can get a prayer through to him."

Aims looks from the folder to Vonder and then asks, "And you think that someone is me?"

With glassy eyes and shaky hands from his weakened condition, but still remaining calm and serious, Vonder says, "I know it is. Can you read this information to me, please?"

Aims stares at Vonder in silence for a moment. Then he pulls a chair up beside Vonder's bed and picks up the folder. He sits down, pulls out his glasses, and starts reading through a stack of papers. Day turns into the late evening as he reads.

Vonder finds out that Pastor Henley was an anointed man of God who prayed a lot. God favored him and blessed him with a special way of touching the lives of others. Pastor Henley believed from the depths of his heart in his special way of winning souls to Christ. He carried it out daily. Vonder learned that Pastor Henley invited people to Christ by praying each morning for God to set up an encounter for him to give a letter to someone for the salvation of that person's soul.

Vonder listened as Aims read about how Pastor Henley always wore a suit coat and kept the invitation letter in his right lapel pocket. He would look an individual directly in the eyes to speak into his soul and hand him the letter, delivering God's invitation to oneness in Christ Jesus.

After reading the entire contents of the folder, Aims reads the newspaper article. The article states that Pastor Henley had that letter in his right lapel pocket at the accident and how the coroner had to move his hand away from his chest on the right side.

As Aims reads the article, Vonder begins to cry. Vonder relives the whole accident over again. He never looked at nor thought about the right lapel pocket. He also realized he was obviously so caught up in himself that he thought Pastor Henley took his last breath, but apparently he hadn't.

Aims read the last portion of the newspaper article. It said:

Mr. Henley was headed south on Highway 16 when a car driving on the wrong side of the road collided head-on with his vehicle. He and the other driver were thrown from their vehicles. The other driver died on impact.

Only one person witnessed the accident. He told police and paramedics Mr. Henley was dead, but paramedics say Mr. Henley regained consciousness after the witness left the scene. He later died at the local emergency room. According to a hospital official, Mr. Henley died with his hand in his right inside lapel pocket, touching an envelope.

His bishop spoke at his services and told a crowd of three hundred how Pastor Henley prayed each morning for God to set him up with someone he could give a letter to accept Christ as their savior.

"He always wore a suit coat and kept the invitation letter in his right lapel pocket. God had gifted him in knowing who was to be the recipient each day. He would look an individual directly in the eyes, get the letter out of his right lapel pocket, and while handing it to them, he would say, 'Take this, it's for you.' His dying with his hand on that right lapel tells me he was inviting someone into oneness with Christ.

"My prayer is that, since they did not receive the letter, they will receive this message. God is still waiting for you," the bishop said as he closed out the service.

Aims stops reading. He looks at Vonder, who is crying profusely, and lays the newspaper article next to Vonder. Aims sits quietly as Vonder releases tears like a waterfall, thinking, *Until the end, Pastor Henley was trying to direct me to his right lapel pocket where God was waiting on me to receive his invitation.*

After a long while, Vonder stops crying and lays still, looking up at the ceiling.

Aims clasps his hands together and begins to pray aloud for Vonder. As Aims prays, Vonder begins to confess his sins.

There is such laboring in prayer that, by the time they are done, Aims says, "I'll check on you in the morning." He pats Vonder on his back and leaves the room.

Vonder is mentally energized by Aims's prayer and his confessing and crying. He is still very weak physically, but he feels like a new man mentally. It is as though the sickness has left his body, even though it is still there. He lies in his hospital bed and prays again.

"Oh God, I have sinned greatly. For me, it's almost too painful to admit. Forgive me, a sinner, Lord; have mercy on my soul. I am broken and wounded. I need and want to have a right relationship with you. Help me, please. I'm ready. What do I need to do?"

Then he, too, feels exhausted. After his prayer, he falls asleep.

Chapter 13
A New Revelation

For the first time since he has been in the hospital, he sleeps through the night.

The next morning, the nurse wakes him for breakfast and asks him if he wants to stay in his room or eat with others in a receiving room.

He almost says no, but he decides he has been isolated too long. He tells her he wants to eat with the others.

She helps him get dressed and rolls him down to the receiving room in a wheelchair.

When he arrives, there is one man sitting in a wheelchair, looking out the window, and one woman in a wheelchair with a younger woman sitting in a chair next to her. They all greet each other, and the room goes silent.

After a while, the younger woman says, "Mom, I brought my CD player and some music for you to listen to while you eat breakfast. I don't know what's taking them so long to bring your food. I'll go check."

"Put the radio on before you go," her mom says. "It's so quiet in here. I don't like it."

Her daughter ask the man sitting next to the window and Vonder if it's okay to turn on the radio. They each nod yes. She turns the radio on and leaves the room to check on breakfast.

After a commercial announcement, a deep voice says, "And now for our early morning spiritual enlightenment, encouragement, and improvement; listen to this new track called 'You Say.'"

Vonder is humbled by the first chorus and the two stanzas he hears, but the words of the last stanza, along with the chorus, pierce his heart.

You know you have those watching, Believing in you all day.
You know you have those asking, 'Is this the Lord's way?'

Now answer from your heart, child; Be true in what you do.
For if you do not answer, sin will destroy you.
I beg of you to stop, now, the things you do and say.
I say to you, 'Stop and turn around,' for now, this is your day.
You need to be a more honest one who leads no one astray.
For what you do in your actions do not match the things that you say.

Vonder tears up and asks the others to please have the aide bring his breakfast to his room. He rolls himself back to his room, sits next to the window, and cries.

Within two days, Vonder is able to sit up all day long.

* * *

After a call from Vonder, Aims announces to the church that he can now receive guests. Albright and Hines tell the congregation they will see Vonder first and let everyone know when to visit so there will be order.

Albright and Hines visit Vonder that day.

At Vonder's hospital bed, Albright says, "I knew God was going to answer the prayers of his people."

"How are you feeling today?" Hines asks.

"Like a saved man," Vonder says.

Albright and Hines respond simultaneously, "What?"

"Like a saved man," he restates his response. "I need the two of you to pick me up and take me to church next Sunday."

"You're sitting up well," Albright says, "but I don't think you should—"

Vonder does not allow him to finish. "Don't think; just trust God. I'll be ready. I need one of you to get some clothes from my house for me."

Albright and Hines look at each other and then back at Vonder.

"I'll get them," Hines says.

Later that week after Bible study, Albright and Hines make their way to the pastor's study and call several of the church members to let them know their pastor will be in church on Sunday.

"Hello, Mother Taylor," Albright says. "Just want you to know your beloved pastor will be in church Sunday."

"Praise the Lord," she says. "I have been praying for the pastor's return, and I know how to get a prayer through. Thank you."

Next, Hines calls Mother Williams.

"Hello, Mother Williams. How are you today?"

"Fine," Mother Williams says. "And you?"

"Just fine," Hines says. "Listen, the pastor will be in church on Sunday."

"Bless God," she says. "Will he preach?"

"Only God knows, Mother," Hines says. "I'll see you on Sunday."

* * *

Still in the hospital, Vonder continues his prayers, and the Holy Spirit continues to speak to him.

Sunday morning arrives, and Albright and Hines bring Vonder into service after praise and worship. They roll his wheelchair to the front of the church. When the congregation sees him, there is pure silence.

Vonder begins, "Good morning, church. Let us pray.

"Father God, be thou exalted from this place, Lord. A few of your humble servants have entered into your house to magnify your name this day. Father, forgive us our sins; cleanse us from all unrighteousness; set us in a right relationship with you. Lord, we acknowledge you as the Lord God Almighty now, always, and forever. Amen."

Vonder lifts his head and continues, "Wisdom, who had long tried to get me to walk in the way of good judgment, was finally able to get God's message into me.

"Some of you may already know there was another pastor on his way to this church to lead you in God's way. He died in a tragic accident. His name was Mr. Henley. Before I met Mr. Henley at the scene of the accident, I was a broken man, not interested in knowing God or seeking his will for my life. I stand before you today a new creation in Christ Jesus. And"—There is a long pause before he continues—"I am not your pastor. I have not been called by God to pastor this church. What God has called me to this earth to do, I do not know. But what is clear to me is that I can know by confessing my sins with a pure heart, as I am doing now. God is faithful and just to forgive and cleanse me from all my sins and unrighteousness.

"I have been praying much for your true pastor to come. I ask that you join me in this prayer. I also ask that you repent of your sins, and let's all pray that we shall have a right relationship with God.

"Finally, I ask that you do not pray that I recover from this sickness but instead focus your prayers on praise to God that I confessed this sin, so that he will spare this entire congregation from the curse I brought upon you. I feel my life will be spared if and only if it is God's will, and I have no desire to be out of God's will, period.

"Now this is the house of the Lord. Since we have entered into his gates, let's continue giving him praise and receive a word from a servant of the Lord. Deacon Aims, will you please bless us with a word from the Lord?"

Vonder positions his wheelchair at the end of the front pew, opens his Bible, and waits for Aims to give a passage of Scripture. Vonder feels the peace of God in the midst of his shame. Until he felt God's peace, he didn't realize he was actually living in turmoil.

Although he does not know what the outcome of his sickness will be, he thinks to himself, *This sickness has blessed me.*

Chapter 14
Religiosity Revealed

Constance, Baryy, and Vonder share a common practice of religiosity—self-centered, pretentious Christianity—while living life on their terms. Although they reaped what they sowed, still God stands at the door of their hearts and knocks.

*   *   *

Vonder stays after service so anyone who wants to speak with him has the opportunity. His main concern is for the healing of the people. Several of the members come to him. Some say nothing; they just look at him and walk away. Some smile while walking past him. Others whisper in his ear and then move on. Still others tell him they knew his confession took a lot and that they love him and will be praying for him. Some turn up their noses at him, and some roll their eyes. But no one is verbally offensive.

After most of the congregation is gone, Ben, one of the youth ministers, comes to him and says, "I'm so proud of you. That could not have been easy. I still respect you as a man and, believe it or not, as a pastor too. This is going to take some time for me to get used to. I think I can speak for the youth as well. Remember, you promised them you were going to support whatever they do."

"I remember," Vonder says, "and I still am—just not as their pastor. Nor am I staying at this church. This church needs to heal. It won't heal with me here. So whatever they do, I'll need you to let me know."

The youth minister agrees, shakes his hand, and says, "Blessings," and then he leaves.

After everyone is gone, Albright and Hines take Vonder back to the hospital. They each want to discuss his confession but are unsure how to even approach the conversation. So they remain quiet. Vonder spends four more days in the hospital and is released with instructions to rest. He follows his doctor's advice and gets plenty of rest. He also starts physical therapy to regain muscle tone.

A member from the church works at the physical therapy center. She sees him there at every session, and they talk. After one session, she sees him leaving and insists on helping him change his diet to eat healthier.

"It's the only way, outside of prayer, for you to recover," she says.

He agrees and follows a strict, healthy eating regimen. Determine to beat his ailment, Vonder makes sure to attend all his strength training sessions and adheres to his healthy diet. As a result, he regains 70 percent of his strength within a three-week period. On Friday evening of his third week, Vonder comes home from his training session and turns his TV to the sports channel to start his weekend of rest and relaxation. While relaxing on his couch, the youth minister calls him.

"Two of the high school boys are in a competition. They asked me to please ask you to come. I'm not supposed to tell you what it is. They want to surprise you."

"Okay," Vonder says. "When?"

"I know this is short notice," Ben says, "but it's tonight. They just told me as well. You know teens."

"I know," Vonder says. "No problem."

"It's casual dress," Ben says. "I'll pick you up at eight."

"I'll be ready," Vonder says.

*   *   *

Constance is glad she has a job, but her bleeding heart has plummeted her into a mild depression.

Spree notices she is not her normal self. One night, she sees Constance totally ignore a customer, who asks about the price of an item she is buying. As Constance is ringing up the items, the customer asks, "I need to know how much this body wash costs. I didn't see a price on the shelf."

Constance never says one word or acknowledges that she even heard the lady. She just continues to ring up the items until she is done, and then she looks at the lady and gives her the total.

After the customer pays and leaves, Spree walks over to Constance and says, "All right. Out with it."

"What?" Constance asks.

"Whatever is eating you," Spree says.

"I told you," Constance says, "I'm fine."

Spree widens her eyes and says, "Hello, I'm an observer as well as a counselor, remember? You just pissed that customer off."

Constance looks shocked.

"Yes," Spree says. "She asked you for the price of that body wash, because she wasn't sure she wanted it, and you just rang it up and ignored her."

"I was thinking about something," Constance explains. "She must have spoken very softly, because I didn't hear her."

"Yeah," Spree says, "so soft that I heard her from my register while you were ringing her up?" She continues, "I hope she doesn't report you; that's how mad she was.

"Now, I know you're Miss Private and all, so I won't ask you again. But I'm telling you, if you don't take a mental break from whatever you're holding in, it's going to destroy you. So I insist you go with me tonight."

"Where? I ... I don't think so," Constance says.

"I didn't ask you," Spree says. "The counselor is insisting, and I will not take no for an answer. What time do you get off? And give me your address; I'll pick you up."

Constance shakes her head, saying no.

"Okay. I know I get off an hour before you. I'll just work until you get off and follow you home."

Quickly, Constance says, "No! I'll meet you here at the store, just tell me what time."

Spree looks at her in disbelief.

"I promise," Constance says.

Spree smiles. "All right," she says. "Eight o'clock."

*   *   *

Baryy's next week is hectic. He is hounded by the police, because Terri is still missing. Charlotte has not decided if she is going to press charges against him for trespassing, so he is full of anxiety because that is still lingering over him. He is mad, because Terri cost him bail money, and he knows he needs a full-time job and fast.

Buddy comes back home the day he bailed Baryy out of jail just in time to see Baryy pulling a can of beer from a twelve-pack.

"Hold up," Buddy says. "No. You're not going down this road. Not here. You're going to deal with this. Now, I like a cold one every now and then. But it's every now and then—mainly during football season when me and the guys share something that size," pointing at the twelve-pack.

127

Baryy is silent. He takes the eleven still in the case and the one he has pulled out and puts them in Buddy's refrigerator.

"Thanks, man," he says.

"I won't say I know what this is like," Buddy says, "but I know how it feels to have your mind messed up. You need a mental break. I know just what you need. Be ready to go at eight o'clock tonight. I'll drive."

Baryy nods. He walks back to his room and closes the door.

Buddy goes to the fridge, takes all twelve cans of beer, and places them in a cabinet in the garage that has a lock on it.

*   *   *

Vonder and Ben, Constance and Spree, and Baryy and Buddy arrive at the local coliseum. The sign on the marquee reads "Experiencing Poetry." Neither of them object to the thought of attending. Once inside, they are all seated near the stage at different round tables. Their three tables are front and center.

All three of them, along with their friends, look at each other and give a warm smile and nod of hello—so common to southern hospitality—as they take their seats. After looking at Baryy, Spree whispers to Constance, "Yes. I'm turned on." After speaking to Spree and Constance, Baryy hopes that the "Grocery Store Honeys" (as he thinks of them) do not approach him. When Baryy and Vonder speak, they each remember bumping into each other at the grocery store.

The reading begins.

The first poets are the two young men from Vonder's old church. They do a great job. The audience stands and applauds.

There are three more poets and then an intermission. Finally the reading starts again, and there are four poets remaining. Three complete their poetry. Constance, Baryy, and Vonder are really enjoying themselves.

The last poet of the night is a beautiful young girl. Unlike the other poets, who gave their names before they started, she walks out onto the stage, positions herself at the microphone, and says simply, "My poem is titled *Pilgrim, Rest.*"

Her voice is smooth, like silk; her words roll off her tongue. Her voice captivates Constance, Baryy, and Vonder, along with the rest of the audience, before she ever begins. Then she begins to recite.

You've traveled your road a long time.

Pilgrim, rest.

Your journey caused agony of heart and mind.

Pilgrim, rest.

Your good you thought was just so great led you to your current fate.

Pilgrim, rest.
Now you're here, Hell's Island marooned.
Pilgrim, rest.
Let your mind tell it, yours is everlasting doom.
Pilgrim, rest.
There is a name above all names,
the One Supreme, he'll never change.
Pilgrim, rest

When the poetess declares, "There is a name above all names, the One Supreme, he'll never change," Constance, Baryy, and Vonder feel a sense of peace, like a refreshing shower. They experience a surge of energy that give them a feeling of wholeness. This was a feeling neither of them had ever felt before.

Her voice grows louder and sharper:

Denounce your doom; bow on your knees; pray! "Christ Jesus! Save me, please!"

She goes silent for a moment and then says with a soft, welcoming voice:

And pilgrim, rest.

She takes her bow.

They want more, but she has softly ended with "And pilgrim. Rest."

After she has so powerfully delivered her message and taken her bow, the only words she speaks are "I invite you all to my church, Pilgrim's Rest Church, where pilgrims rest. We are located on Eighth Street. God bless you."

Then she stares at Constance, Baryy, and Vonder as though God is looking at them, giving them warm, loving invitations to come out of the wilderness and into his rest. She then turns and leaves the stage, without giving her name.

They long to see her when the poetry reading is over. They look diligently for her when the audience meets the poets, but she is nowhere to be found. All they have to cling to is the thought that she has invited them to Pilgrim's Rest Church on Eighth Street.

Epilogue

The very next Sunday morning after the poetry reading, Constance Wilts, Baryy Greene, and Vonder Staten walk through the entrance of Pilgrim's Rest Church on Eighth Street.

They each come alone. They remember each other from the poetry reading and greet one another while standing in the church vestibule. The church greeters welcome them, and the ushers escort them to the same pew.

They are no strangers to church service. The question is: Is this just another service? Or have the selfish decided to take the road of the selfless to become servants? When the alter call is made, one of them joins the church ...

Coming Soon!
Perpetrator 2

"When Constance, Baryy and Vonder lives plummeted them into despair, they knew, only God, through His Holy Spirit, could help them fix their mess. And for a while their mess, got messier.

But in reality, they were on the verge of life experiences that would change them for the better, forever".

To learn more go to www.perpetratorbook.com, or email: vernel@perpetratorbook.com